Praise for Atlantis Under Siege

"A beautiful book by a young author with a promising future, focused on humanity, tolerance and other purposeful meanings, and emphasized principles and values that people need in every time and place "today and in 2064"."

- His Excellency Turki A. Aldakhil
Kingdom of Saudi Arabia Ambassador to the United Arab Emirates

"Riyah's compelling arguments to save the world from the disastrous consequences of Climate Change has been superbly captured in an enthralling sci-fi story that flows like poetry all along. Highly recommended for the young and old. Read it to immerse yourself on a journey below the sea and save the world when you come upon land."

- Faisal Farooqui

Entrepreneur, Founder of MouthShut.com

"On reading the book, it was clear to me that Riyah is a gifted soul. At the tender age of 15, she displays clarity and maturity through her writing, making the book a masterpiece. She beautifully describes the importance of being an empath to which I strongly agree. I have always been a believer of giving people more than what they expect. Overall, this book is her crowning achievement."

- Dr. Ali Irani

Celebrity Physiotherapist, Indian Cricket Team Physiotherapist

"The book, Atlantis Under Siege, is a power-packed punch to open our eyes, to understand that the time has come to wake up to the reality that we must protect the earth, so we can all live and flourish in it, with sympathy, empathy, and compassion for all."

- Dr. Mickey Mehta
Global Leading Holistic Health Guru

"A very beautiful story which has a simple yet strong message of love for the environment and all living beings. While it paints a brutally honest picture about the mistakes made, it also has unending hope for the goodness of human beings and for the future. A wonderful read for all ages."

- Suhaas Shetty
Screenwriter and Director

"A brilliantly told story that relentlessly pulls you in and doesn't let you go till the last unexpected twist. It got me so hooked I couldn't put it down. This tribute will bring tears as well as a much needed reminder that saving the earth is not an option but a necessity for our survival. It's one of those few books that makes you laugh, cry and learn so much. A must read for all ages."

- Shehzad Khan
Bollywood Actor

ATLANTIS UNDER SIEGE

ATLANTIS UNDER SIEGE

RIYAH GANI

RIGI PUBLICATION

RIGI PUBLICATION

ATLANTIS UNDER SIEGE

BY

RIYAH GANI

Originally published in India

ISBN: 978-93-91041-69-4

Published by RIGI PUBLICATION

Printer: Manipal Printers

777, Street no.9, Krishna Nagar

Khanna-141401 (Punjab), India

Website: www.rigipublication.com

Email: info@rigipublication.com

Phone: +91-9357710014, +91-9465468291

To

The fragile oceans, whose survival depends on the conscience of mankind

We think too much and feel too little. More than machinery, we need humanity; more than cleverness, we need kindness and gentleness. Without these qualities, life will be violent and all will be lost.

-Charlie Chaplin

FOREWORD

Atlantis Under Siege is a beautiful story set in 2064, where air: oxygen is the most expensive commodity on the planet after fresh water. It then flashbacks to a time when the protagonist is a young girl, living in the present times we live in and portends a tale of how human greed ebbs the very fundamental things we need to survive as humans! The book is a 'not so subtle' reminder of our abusive relationship with Mother Nature.

In an uncanny way, it has a bit of Greta Thunberg in the plot and the storytelling is akin to the Titanic keeping you engaged and engrossed right from the first chapter.

A group of sailors get marooned on an island, struggle to survive, and get saved by the creatures of the ocean that have always known to be the friends of human beings, helping them out in their adversity. But as time goes by, humans turn traitors to the very ocean that supports us.

Our machiavellian side takes over, destroying the planet's ecosystem which in turn, due to our greed and short-sightedness, brings us humbling to our knees, gasping for breath, a nostradamian reminder of the times to come!

Riyah's story telling is fast-paced gripping and though black and white, mincing no words, yet she gives the reader enough metaphors, transporting us into three-dimensional structures of light and sound, conjuring up the scenes in its vibrant colours.

Riyah's style of writing is fresh, spirited, lucid and eloquent that very few of her age can boast of.

From a young student of Dance in my Institute to now a budding writer, Riyah lets her pen dance effortlessly, choreographing a rich narrative with a thought-provoking message! A powerful pen especially in the hands of one so young and able, is truly admirable and makes for a good read to be enjoyed by all ages!

-Dr. Terence Lewis

Internationally acclaimed Choreographer and TV Judge

PREFACE

The Pandemic changed our lives in so many ways; particularly my outlook towards life and our environment. It opened my eyes and made me realise the value of the smaller things in life that we invariably overlook. I was compelled to pen down my thoughts. What emerged was a riveting story about friendship, trust, deception and betrayal and how compassion, love and humanity for all creatures transcends darkness.

ACKNOWLEDGEMENT

I am extremely grateful to His Excellency Turki A. Aldakhil for the positive encouragement and kind words.

I would sincerely like to thank Dr. Ali Irani, Mr. Faisal Farooqui, Mr. Shehzad Khan, Dr. Mickey Mehta and Mr. Suhaas Shetty for patiently reading my manuscript and giving me your invaluable feedback, support and encouragement.

Terence sir for the positive attitude and vibrance that you envelop everybody in and the grit to follow your passion that I have imbibed from you. Thank you.

All my teachers, thank you for inspiring me and motivating me through the years. Especially Jestin sir, this book would not be possible without your guidance and mentoring.

Thank you to the entire team of Rigi Publications for believing in my book Atlantis Under Siege and helping my dream become a reality.

And lastly, thank you to my amazing mother, for your love and support in all my endeavours, for inspiring me to love reading as much as you do and for filling our house with books I could fall in love with. My wonderful father, for your love and unwavering belief in me and the encouragement to pursue my dreams. You truly are and will always be the wind beneath my wings. My sister Alayna, for patiently listening to the many drafts of Atlantis Under Siege and for being my truest critique. Thank you.

The list is incomplete without mentioning my wonderful friends, thank you for your constant love and support!

CONTENTS

PROLOGUE

I wake up to the morning sunlight filtering through my expansive white windows. As the first rays of the sun hit the window, the blinds start to disappear, till my room is completely lit.

Stretching, I sit up in bed, rubbing my eyes, and reach out for my smart glasses. "Good morning Lyra, today is August eighteenth, 2064. The weather is a scorching 50 degrees, have a great day!" the pleasant voice cuts off with a beep.

Still yawning, I get out of bed and face a full-length mirror. Forty-four years have passed and a lot has changed. The world has made technological advancements and AI has taken over, but our lives have taken a turn for the worse- I haven't inhaled a breath of fresh air for the longest time. My hair has turned river silver. The ebb and flow of time has chiselled my face, leaving it as crinkly as faded parchment, but the twinkle in my eye and the desire to live still flares as brightly as a star flame. My memory is as sharp as tack, even now.

Xander X, my humanoid robot, comes over and hands me three meal pills with a glass of water. Two eggs, toast, and a glass of juice, down my throat in less than a minute! I walk into a small room and within seconds, I am clean. Showering is not a thing anymore, we have very little fresh water left.

Following my daily routine, I decide to go for a walk by the beach. At the moment of decision, my clothes intelligently reshape themselves onto my body, becoming sweat-absorbent and optimized for comfortable walking.

I put my smart glasses back on, they measure my heart rate and pulse and warn me that today is not a good day for a walk as the oxygen levels are likely to remain low and that there is a fifty per cent chance of acid rain, but I can't not go.

My love for the ocean has not diminished, and not a single day goes by without me visiting the beach, listening to the waves, even though the ocean has now more plastic than water, and marine life has dwindled to almost negligible. I still love living by the ocean, but most people I know have moved out. In my mind's eye, I see my younger self, standing at the beach, facing the water and the sun, the salty air tousling my hair and rippling the cloth of my T-shirt. I blink, and then it's gone, one memory amongst a thousand others.

Before I leave, Xander hands me my oxygen hood, a transparent sphere that I quickly put on. It's too dangerous to step out without it. Oxygen levels fluctuate to a great extent and can fall very low, today, again, and what was for the third time in one week, was going to be that kind of day.

I walk to the beach slowly, my speed is not quite like it used to be. I stroll in the meagre strip of sand that is left behind after the sea levels rose and watch the powerful rolling waves and shifting tides. The sun shines brightly overhead. I dig my shoe into the sand and think about my childhood, the clean waters in which my friends and I would swim, the colourful marine life that existed within.

At a distance, I see a crowd gathered at the shoreline, they're standing in a tight group, ogling at something that just washed up. I couldn't see what it was.

Curiosity spiked, I hurry closer. A young boy tugs on his mother's sleeve, inquiring about the dead creature lying on the sand. Reporters don't take too long to arrive. The story is momentous even if the takeaway isn't very pleasant.

Everyone knows there used to be fish in the oceans–sort of like those that are sometimes seen in a few lakes and rivers, except- they were way larger, as well as more diverse and even more colourful. But those ocean fish had all died. Except maybe this one. This one was alive in there, and now it's gone too.

My breath hitched when I saw the creature, what lay before me looked less like a fish and more like a puffy, leathery grey blotch on the sand. It had a long needle-like snout. With a gasp I realize what it is- a swordfish; but instead of its iridescent silver skin there was this. *What was going on under the water?*

I hoped that there would be more fish- healthy ones, still surviving in the depths where humans hadn't been able to venture. I couldn't bear to look at it any longer, I quickly made my way back home, thinking about what this meant for us as humans.

Just as I had reached home and settled into my couch, the doorbell buzzed and Xander answered. To my surprise, standing at the door were my four grandchildren- Ilaria, Verina, Kasper, and Valory- the youngest. "Gran!" They yell joyfully from the doorway, before attacking me with bear hugs.

I am momentarily distracted from the devastating morning incident as I welcome them with their favourite snack- fresh baked cookies with milk, a rarity nowadays, with all the food pills, but they love it. Verina switches on the television and it is displayed on the wall. As she flips through the channels, an image of the swordfish that had washed up on-shore is displayed.

A lady with a bob shakes her head mournfully, "The last remaining species of fish in the ocean was found dead today. I believe no marine life exists anymore."

I'm too stunned to move. *This shouldn't be happening, no! It can't be possible, how could we have lost all marine life?* "Gran!" Kasper shook my knee, interrupting my musings. "Gran!" he squealed, hopping from one foot to another, "Look what I found!" he waves an old, worn-looking black diary in front of my face and a picture falls out. As he leans down to pick it up, I recognize the diary.

I take it from his hands, run my hand across the now worn-out hide, carefully open it, and turn its yellow pages. I turn the pages, going back in time. A gentle breeze plays with my hair as I lean from the edge of my boat, peering at a shoal of fish. The salty sea mist envelopes my senses and I let out a carefree laugh.

A tap on my shoulder brings me back to reality. I hold the diary close to my chest, my shoulders slump and tears slip down my cheeks as pangs wreck my heart. Flustered and confused by my reaction, the young children want to know the reason behind those tears.

Xander prepares steaming mugs of hot chocolate, as the children settle onto the couch, anxious to hear my story. I sink into my armchair and open the diary with trembling hands once again. I trace my fingers across the faded writing and old pictures, which bring back a flood of memories.

The year 2020 had been full of turmoil, the death and economic devastation that it brought with it was unprecedented and snowballed to affect the entire world.

Plans were disrupted and high-strung emotions played to the hilt bringing the world to a grinding halt. As I think about those times, it brings back the challenges we faced and how we managed to navigate through them and emerged stronger, humbler and united.

"As advanced as we thought we were, a tiny microscopic virus was more than capable of creating havoc in our lives. It was called the Novel Corona Virus, more commonly known as the Covid 19."

"What was the cause of the virus Gran?" asked Verina.

"It began with an outbreak of respiratory illnesses and was rumoured to have come in contact with humans because an infected bat was eaten."

"People didn't think much of it until it began to make them seriously ill. On January 30, 2020, the WHO declared the COVID-19 outbreak a global health emergency and on March 11, 2020, a global pandemic."

"The death tolls had surged. The illness had taken millions of lives in its wake and not a single country was spared. Almost every single person had lost someone they loved. Soon enough lockdowns were introduced, streets wore a deserted look, the bustling restaurants and shops, schools, colleges, government offices, private corporates, industries, all shut down operations within a few days, bringing everything to a standstill.

The lockdowns seemed endless as governments of even the most developed countries could only wait in anticipation for the situation to improve while they watched their economies suffer. This caused a vast majority of people to lose their livelihood and brought quite a few to the brink of poverty.

As months passed, governments started to find measures to contain the virus, some faster than others. Work and study from home were first experimented with and implemented in a big way. Something you find normal now. Masks, gloves and sanitisers coupled with temperature checks were the new normal. Social distancing norms were put in place, no one could meet and greet like before, no hugs, no handshakes. This improved the condition for a while and then the virus hit back again, stronger and harder.

People had lost all hope but a few; healthcare workers were busy saving lives and scientists developing a vaccine to get the world back on its feet. Sure enough, the vaccine worked, with a rapid three-phased trial. The deadly virus was finally contained to some extent and people learned to live with it.

Lives of the people slowly improved; however, it was never going to be the same again for many." The younger children looked at me bewildered, but the eldest one, Ilaria, perked up and said, "I studied about it in middle school, you will too. They were the toughest times humanity had faced but had fought against all odds and emerged a winner. Right Gran?" I smiled and nodded my head just the slightest and flipped another page.

As I turned the pages, I could smell its faint, yet sweet and musky fragrance. I saw a picture of me and two of my best friends, Alessia and Zane at a beach, kneeling in the sand with Frisky, our green sea turtle friend, who had unfortunately passed away a few years ago due to suffocation by plastic waste thrown into the sea. Zane and Alessia had married and moved to Europe.

Another picture was of a pod of dolphins in the sea. Below it, in neat uppercase letters, were the words, "*MISSION ACCOMPLISHED.*" I smiled and reflected, as much as mankind struggled, nature flourished. "We had clear blue skies. Sea and river pollution were at their lowest, animals were living in absolute freedom and plants were blossoming.

But one thing had not changed: human greed, it could not be bound by nature's fury. Some people did not pay heed to the warnings or try to understand how fragile our ecosystem was and that we needed to preserve it, even when there were more than enough warning signs- *four hundred* natural calamities and a virus that completely upturned our lives had hit the world in a span of a year alone, but even that, did nothing to make them understand the importance of coexistence. Unfortunately, greed and deception had found their way even in those tough times, for which we have all paid a heavy price. The greed of a few has robbed us of our basic life support - oxygen."

"So what did you do to save the Earth, Gran? Did you bring the bad guys to their heels and defeat them?" said Val, looking at me with her big almond-shaped eyes, almost pleading. I shied away and muttered in a whisper, "No my dear, I couldn't stop them, even though I tried my best."

1

THE DARK MIRROR

A plastic sheet. A young dolphin. Suffocating. Another dolphin- Claire, watched, frozen with shock at the gruesome sight, helpless to act, as her best friend Elle met a slow and painful end.

* * *

Elle and I had been best friends since childhood. Actually- we were more than just that. She was not related to me by blood, that much is true, but a bond as special as ours ran way deeper than blood, if truth be told.

Both our mothers had been a part of a clique wherein many dolphins who shared similar interests gathered together. It was a relatively large clique with plenty of other dolphins and several such cliques existed within our pod. Our mothers met each other for the first time during one such gathering and had grown so close that they were literally inseparable.

As we grew older, our mothers would take us to different areas of the sea and teach us various kinds of tricks to catch prey.

One day as we hunted for the more nutritious fish that were hiding within the sandy seabed, Elle received a rather nasty scratch on her rostrum. This led to us learning about fishing tools, well, it was mainly sponging.

We learned from our mothers how a sea sponge could come in extremely handy to plough through the abrasive and rocky sands without hurting ourselves. It was as easy as placing one of them on our rostras! Elle chose a flaming red coloured sea sponge, placed it on her rostrum and did a funny dance, urging me to do the same, we all laughed, that's just how perky she always was. I looked around and a sunny yellow sponge caught my eye. It was easy enough to pluck it out, and I held on tightly while digging through the sand. It protected my rostra well enough, but by the time the fish darted out, I was completely breathless and unable to catch it.

My mother watched me as I tried again- and failed. She saw my disgruntled expression and patted my head lovingly. She told me not to worry and then explained that there was a trick to it.

Demonstrating, she grabbed a sponge and dislodged the fish from its hiding place, I watched her intently, while it took the disturbed fish some time to go back into hiding, my mother swam up to the surface, took a quick breath of air and dove back to catch the fish. I clapped my hands in glee! This quick demonstration was all that was needed before Elle and I managed to get the fish. These sea sponges protected our snouts from abrasive materials and enabled us to dig easily into the sandy seafloor. We also saw some shrimps crawling around and cheerfully indulged in them. What a treat! The area we were in was shallow and humans peered at us from their glass-bottomed boats pointing and waving excitedly. We were quite used to seeing them around and so carried on with our day, unperturbed.

* * *

One day, as we went on with our routine in a state-protected area of the sea where fishing was banned for humans, we were all engrossed in trying to catch some prey and completely missed some carefully planted illegal fishing nets that the humans had left behind. Before we knew it, we were entangled in its clutches. We were trapped like a fly in a jar, thrashing wildly to get free. But alas! Nothing we did could free us.

My mother was the only one swimming far enough not to be caught in the net. As soon as she saw us trapped, she desperately rushed towards us, not fearing for her own safety. She tried extremely hard to rip it off us but the net was just too strong. We strained against it but it was like pushing against a brick wall, utterly useless.

"Claire! Clairee!!"

"Huh!"

"What is it?" Elle asked, "Why aren't you pushing against the net anymore?"

"Look!" I mouthed wordlessly, gesturing towards a white blob in the distance.

Colour drained from her face like heat drains from lake water in the midst of the winter freeze over. As it came closer, I saw that it was a

Great White Shark. *Ugh!* I shuddered inwardly, these guys were super dangerous. They usually avoided us, but today we were far away from the pod and trapped in a net.

The shark was coming closer and closer. Its dark eyes were full of endless hostility. Fear gripped me with its icy fingers, I pushed against the net frantically, but it refused to budge.

Looking at our gaze fixed into the distance, our mothers realized that the net was not the only danger we were in, there was something more dangerous not too far off. They too had spotted the great white and had kept their composure, working even more strenuously, pulling at the net from both sides, hoping to tear it, and we tried our best to help them.

A nervous tremor ran through Elle's body. Our mothers spoke to each other in soft, low tones. Elle's mother's brows furrowed and she became extremely distressed. She paced the length of the net as my mother came over to us and told us that we would be fine but we needed to keep extremely silent and stay as still as possible. She gave me a reassuring tap and dropped a kiss on my forehead. "Everything's going to be alright, don't worry," she said, and then started to swim away. Elle's mother desperately held on to her, trying to block her path but she broke free of her grasp. The shark was *really* fast, it had almost reached us and was boring holes into our skin with its gaze.

Elle's mother kept shaking her head and softly whispering "No" as my mother moved further away from us. She splashed her tail to grab the shark's attention. I could only watch, transfixed in horror, as the shark looked at us, hesitated, and then turned its head towards my mother and sped after her. She swam swiftly and raced ahead of the shark. It followed her into the distance. "*BOOM!!*" Shrinking away from the noise, I covered my ears.

I don't remember much after that. I felt a strong stabbing sensation at the back of my head. I heard Elle scream- but it seemed to come from far away. Everything was happening in slow motion. I saw blood mixed with water swirling around. Large rocks, bits of coral, seaweed, and marine life floated past us. I felt my vision going black. A sharp piece of rock tore the net and we were free.

Immediately, Elle's mother warned us to stay put and rushed in the direction that we had seen my mother go. As we waited for her to come back I drifted in and out of consciousness. I had hazy visions of Elle dragging me to the surface for breaths of air.

I don't know how long we waited, but when Elle's mother came back, she had tears streaming down her face. She looked at me with sorrow and regret in her eyes and told me that my mother was no more.

My face crumpled and I felt like I was drowning in quicksand. A heavy weight was crushing my body. I wanted to scream, but no sound would come out. Salty tears rolled down my cheeks as I sobbed uncontrollably, it felt as though someone had stabbed me with a knife and was twisting it slowly, painfully. As if the pain of losing my mother wasn't enough, I was staring into a black abyss of life without any family, the life of an orphan.

There would be no one to teach me how to catch prey, or protect me from monstrous predators. Elle too, was in tears. She hugged me tightly and tried to comfort me. I sagged against her.

The words that Elle's mother had told me that day as she wiped away tears that wouldn't stop flowing, were etched in my heart forever. She opened her arms to me and I went to her, gratefully.

She said somberly, "I know that I'll never be able to take the place of your mother, but I want you to know that you will always be my daughter." And she was true to her word. She never, ever, treated me any different from Elle.

* * *

For a very long time, I didn't know how my mother had died. Elle's mother blatantly refused to answer every time I asked. It was only after many years when we had grown older and were on one of our expeditions, we saw some humans dive into the sea. They seemed to be looking for something specific and we followed them at a safe distance.

One of them spotted a black spherical structure lying on the sea bed, he then motioned to the others and they all quickly got to work, collecting it carefully. I'd seen some of these before. They were all over the place.

The men had found some more of them and were working hard, cautiously picking them up. Once each and every one of the circular *things* had been picked up, they swam back to the surface where a large boat pulled them up. I trailed behind them, leaving Elle behind.

Once the man was on board I heard him say, "Fred, I have been uncovering these demons for ages now, hoping they do not harm any more sea creatures," he went on to explain how these mines were live and how they exploded, how they had taken countless innocent lives of humans and fish alike.

After losing his son, he had dedicated his life to uncovering the mines and making the sea safe for all. Finally, realization dawned on me, they were bombs called sea mines, left in the depths of the sea from previous human wars. I pictured the loud blast and the destruction from that day, related it to the human talk, and understood that it was this explosion that had taken the life of that menacing shark and my mother, leaving me an orphan. Though the knowledge gave me some closure about her death, though it did not make the pain any less. I silently swam back to Elle.

II

Elle and I had always regarded each other as sisters and did everything together. We explored the sea, blew bubble rings, followed in the wake of ships, socialized, surfed waves and caught prey together. It was as though we were joined at the hip!

* * *

Once, when we had gone to the surface for a breath of air, we saw that a shiny red boat had overturned and its occupants had been cast adrift. The humans seemed to be doing okay, but among them was a dog who was clearly terrified of the water. It was making a series of high-pitched yelps. Its large brown eyes pleaded for help as it splashed around looking for something to hold on to. Its long golden hair was soaking water like a sponge and the weight would soon drown it. Still, it was trying its best, paddling desperately to keep afloat.

Elle and I looked at each other, making a split-second decision, we decided to save it. We swam close to the dog and it thankfully clambered onto my back, but its paws were wet and slippery and it soon started to slip off, falling back into the water. If the humans were close, they would have possibly heard its petrified whines and come to its aid, but they were too far away.

Elle and I got the dog in between both of us and somehow managed to get it to hold on. With its nervous paws around our dorsal fins and neck craned to keep its head above the waterline, we swam the dog to the safety of its owners who had succeeded in getting back onto the boat.

They gratefully pulled the dog over the edge. The dog perked up almost instantly, straightening its droopy ears and wagging its tail joyfully. As soon as it was upon all fours, it shook itself, sending a spray of water into the air. It then leaned towards the water and licked us both in turn. Perhaps that was its way of saying thank you. It watched us as we swam away and gave us a short bark just before we disappeared under the water.

Elle and I never shied away from helping creatures in need and always tried our best to aid them in whatever way possible.

* * *

On one occasion, we visited a sunken ship at a secret location that one of our friends had told us about.

We timidly approached the enormous vessel that sprawled over the ocean floor. Circling the ship, we saw faded letters on its side that read, "*THE DRAKON KHOLKIKOS*" which we assumed was the name that was given to her by her human owners when she was built.

She was not in the best of shape, counting the fact that she had a large hole on her starboard side hull and several shattered windows. The cold, salty waters had seemingly gotten the best of her, and, from a distance, she looked worn out and tired, like she knew the grand life that she had been made for would never be hers again. Orange-brown-coloured rust invaded the areas where the paint had chipped, giving the obsidian black ship a reddish glow in certain areas. Not much remained of the tiny details that once made her stand out, they had either eroded or faded away over time. Only faint traces remained in some places.

The bow of the ship housed its massive figurehead. It was shielded from view by the curtains of kelp and sea lettuce that had inhabited the dilapidated ship. Even with all the life covering it, you couldn't mistake it for anything other than what it was- A magnificent dragon. It was made of pure gold that had not rusted or decayed in the slightest. It had seemingly lasted forever, as though it were immortal. The magnetic aura of the glistering beast called out to us, drawing us closer and closer.

As we approached it, Elle's tail lightly brushed past its face. At that moment, we heard a low, deep, earthy roar. Startled, we wondered what it was all about, and then we noticed that the emerald green eyes of the dragon were emanating a soft glow that increased in intensity.

A commanding voice reverberated around us, "Who calls upon the mighty Kholkikos?" Elle and I looked around, but there was no one there except us. So who could have spoken? Nervously, I looked toward the dragon and blurted, "Did you just speak?" Elle gave me a look that said she thought I had lost it.

We turned around once again to look at the dragon. Its eyes had stopped glowing and had become completely gold. It lifted its eyelids to reveal its iridescent eyes. The eyes were so exquisite, they left me breathless, they were softly woven with a chorus of green threads, the green of every forest, liquid and alive.

We were completely mesmerized, frozen in place like a block of ice as we looked on with awe. "Yesss" it hissed. We were shocked beyond words and remained riveted. The dragon bellowed, "Do not be afraid, I shall not harm you. But it has been a long time since I had a visitor. No one has called upon me for centuries."

"Oh!" I murmured softly.

Elle mustered up the courage and asked, "What are you? How can you speak?"

The dragon replied, "I am Kholkikos, an enchanted figurehead, made from pure gold."

"We can see that," I muttered, rolling my eyes. This dragon was quite a show-off, it seemed.

Elle nudged me in the ribs, telling me to shut up.

"I was destined to be a storyteller and keep the sailors on the ship entertained so as to not lose heart as they travelled on perilous quests and sailed through treacherous waters and storm-filled days." The dragon continued. "I have been named after the ever awake, immense serpent, The Kholkikos Drakon. It was said to never sleep, rest, or lower its vigilance. In ancient Greek mythology, it was said to have guarded the legendary Golden Fleece in a grove sacred to Ares in Kolkhis."

"How interesting!" I exclaimed, now over my initial dislike.

"Would you like to hear the tale?" the golden dragon proposed joyously.

"Yes, yes," Elle and I blurted in unison.

III

"Long ago," began the joyful dragon in a deep voice that was very easy on the ears, "In the ancient Greek city of Iolcus, lived a wicked man named Pelias.

Pelias had killed Aeson, his brother and the real king, and taken his throne; but lived in constant fear of being overthrown by Aeson's descendants. Aeson's wife, in a bid to keep Jason, her son and the rightful king of Iolcus, safe, smuggled him out of the city as a baby sent him away to be brought up by Chiron, a mighty centaur- half man, half horse.

Chiron was known for his wisdom and strength; so Jason grew up to be a strong and smart young man. As Jason grew older, he became a formidable warrior and, when he reached adulthood, he set out to reclaim his rightful throne from Pelias.

When he reached Iolcus, he was greeted by a furious Pelias, who demanded that Jason prove himself as a capable king by setting off on a quest to find the Golden Fleece, a mythical fleece from a winged ram."

"So what does he do?" asked Elle.

"Jason agrees, and sets out on his ship, The Argo, with his crew of Argonauts that included heroes like Heracles, Orpheus, Castor, Pollux and Atalanta, the only female to have participated in the hunt.

On their journey, Jason and the Argonauts reach the court of Phineus, king of Salmydessus in Thrace, who is also a seer. Phineus describes to the hero how he is tormented by the Harpies, who defile his food whenever he tries to eat.

"That sounds horrible," I exclaimed. "Do they help him?" Elle chimed in.

"Yes. Among the Argonauts are Phineus' brothers-in-law, the Boreads, who help him and chase the Harpies away for good. In return, Phineus informs them how to safely pass through the Symplegades, a pair of huge rock cliffs that clash together to crush things that go past them, in order to reach Colchis.

The journey is arduous, but the Argonauts make it.

The fleece itself is owned by King Aeetes of Colchis who promises to give it to Jason if he completes three tasks.

He must yoke fire-breathing bulls, plough and sow a field with the teeth of the dragon guarding the Fleece and then overcome the warriors who will rise from the furrows.

Aeetes is confident that the tasks are impossible but unbeknownst to the king, his daughter Medea, a powerful sorceress, takes a liking to Jason and offers to assist him if he agrees to marry her. He agrees, and completes all the tasks with her help.

After successfully retrieving the Fleece, they sail home to Iolcus and Jason presents it to Pelius. The king refuses to give up his throne and so, Medea has him killed by his own daughters.

Jason and Medea are then exiled to Corinth where the King of Corinth offers Jason his daughter's hand in marriage. Jason agrees and so violates his vow to the gods to be true only to Medea.

Enraged, Medea kills the woman, her children with Jason, and then ascends to Mount Olympus where she eventually marries Achilles.

Jason goes back to Iolcus where he finds his ship, The Argo. As he sits under the ship, a decaying beam falls on his head and kills him."

I let out a sigh, "What a tragic end!" Elle shakes her head sorrowfully in agreement.

The dragon then says, "If you come back tomorrow, I'll tell you another story."

"Please, just one more," we begged the dragon.

The mythical creature agreed, though somewhat reluctantly. We were all ears as the tale began, "Perhaps the most terrifying sea monster of all is the Kraken.

A tale originating from the frightened whispers of Scandinavian seamen, this huge mass of tentacles was believed to be capable of taking down entire ships in its many-armed embrace.

When it was hungry, the leviathan would release a substance made of its previous meals into the water. This acted as bait and would cause impressive amounts of fish to flock to the area.

After the Kraken felt enough fish had gathered, it would rise to the surface and devour them all, then fall into a deep sleep while it digested the food.

Soon sailors realized that the fish were drawn to a particular area at certain times when the Kraken was feeding, so they attempted to sail overhead and drop their nets in order to skim off of the Kraken's food source.

As soon as the Kraken realized that sailors were stealing bites from his meals, he grew upset, and that caused him to sink the ships and eat the sailors.

Whenever a ship tried to rob food from the giant - or bothered it in general -it would create a massive whirlpool and raise its tentacles out of the water to capsize the vessel in question."

"Whoa! The Kraken sounds really dangerous" I murmured, while Elle said, "What the sailors did was quite mean too. Imagine someone taking away bits of the food that you've been waiting for."

The dragon replied, "You have been listening well little ones. One cannot say that only the Kraken is at fault in this story, for it was only retaliating against the sailors who were stealing its food."

The ancient dragon added, "Well, it is now time for me to slumber, so go along on your way and when you come back, I shall regale you with more tales of mystery and magic."

IV

We bade the dragon farewell and decided to look around. The crates and containers of various sizes strewn all around would probably tell you of the treasures the ship housed on its final voyage but there was nothing inside the ones that had broken open.

There were no signs of human remains, so you could assume that they'd made it out alive, but the watery domain might have claimed them a long time ago.

It was quite daunting to step inside and explore her completely, but curiosity got the better of us and we began to look around.

Even the hardest places to reach had corals growing in them and they housed all kinds of colourful fish. Just as deserted and dead as it looked on the outside was it alive and thriving on the inside. It was a whole new world in there!

We went up and down the impressive staircases, peeking into the spacious rooms with lofty ceilings and king-sized beds. There was no doubt in our minds that she was once a magnificent liner that hosted grand voyagers.

Its evidence lay in the grand halls, intricate patterns in the walls, torn fabrics that were once fine linens and chipped porcelain sets. In some rooms, we saw carved wooden tables set with random bits of fine crockery and shiny silver cutlery. Old, rotting, cushioned chairs were strewn around.

Elle and I found and ate plenty of delectable fish, shrimp and squid. After we had our fill, we explored some more. We played hide and seek in the tall seagrass that was growing on the upper deck and were joined by a lone shark pup that had made the shipwreck its home.

We also met our turtle friends Lunar, a leatherback turtle, and Frisky, a green sea turtle, as we were leaving. They told us that this was the perfect place to get the finest and freshest food as these corals remained largely undisturbed by visitors.

The prey had plenty to eat and could thrive and grow peacefully without having to think about being someone's next meal. That had made them exceedingly carefree and in addition to being highly nutritious, they were easier to catch due to fewer encounters with predators.

Lunar loved eating gelatinous invertebrates like jellyfish and sea squirts and Frisky only ate algae and seagrass. Lunar laughed and said, "Never mind what you eat, this ship is the best feeding ground as it provides you with everything you could possibly ever desire."

While Frisky showed us how he scraped algae from the rocky corals Lunar told us to wait for a while and swam off. He returned after a few minutes and ushered us along to one of the lower decks.

We stopped in front of a large wooden door that was rotting away at the hinges. Elle looked at me with raised eyebrows and a questioning look, I shrugged and gave her a slight frown. I had *no* idea what Lunar was up to.

The turtles pushed heavily against the door and it came down with a loud *crash.* A shower of sand rained down on us. We stepped inside slowly, careful not to let the small splinters of wood pierce our delicate skin.

What we saw there, left our mouths hanging open. Several hundreds of medusae, countless blooms of them circled us. Each one was no bigger than the nail on a human's pinkie finger.

Crystal clear bells with fiery red stomachs and iridescent shimmering tentacles floated lazily past us. It was an extremely rare sight! Never had I ever imagined that I'd be seeing so many of the *Immortal Jellyfish* in one place.

Elle and I were over the moon. We had only heard stories about them from the elders. They had been termed immortal because they had the unique ability to regenerate and go back to the plankton stage even after reaching maturity. The only way they could die was by being eaten, getting a disease, or by being taken out of water.

While Elle and I stared at them, *oohing* and *ahhing* in wonder, with the biggest smiles on our faces, Lunar, tired of watching our reactions, had started to gobble them one by one.

He caught us glaring at him and gestured for us to try some for ourselves. Staring at him incredulously, we refused.

He shrugged and carried on, but watching him smack his lips made our stomachs rumble. Finally, our desire to taste them got the better of us and we gave up on trying to control ourselves. Lunar smirked as we ate and Frisky stood watching. They were truly the most delicious jellyfish I had ever tried in my life.

V

Elle and I would frequently make our way into uncharted waters for the sake of an adventure.

* * *

Once, we were swimming through an unfamiliar region, chasing an electric ray. Elle raced ahead, leaving me quite far behind as she went after it.

I called out to her, wanting and urging her to wait until I caught up with her, but there was no response. I could barely catch a glimpse of her tail. She was too engrossed in trying to catch the ray.

I can never forget that fateful day, as I watched from a distance when all of a sudden, the ray disappeared, and in its place appeared a glistening sheet of plastic.

I let out a screech trying to warn her but she was swimming so quickly that she couldn't stop herself from crashing into it and the plastic sheet wrapped itself around her.

She thrashed wildly in its unrelenting clutches but it made no difference at all, the plastic sheet had gripped her too tightly.

On seeing her thrash around, I swam faster, with all my might and tried to reach her, but alas! I was too slow. I couldn't save the one who had always been there for me.

With a violent shudder, Elle went completely still and I watched the little forlorn shadows dart across her body as it sank to the bottom of the deep blue. I had lost my only companion.

I dimly heard a guttural wail, and realized with a start that I was the one making the noise. The pain was unbearable, images flashed through my mind, Elle laughing, both of us at the surface watching the sunset, Elle hugging me, comforting me, all the moments we spent together spiralling into each other as I embraced the wave of darkness that was settling over me.

2

GIVE THEM A CHANCE

Claire's eyes shot open, her forehead was clammy with sweat and vivid images danced before her. The same dream was haunting her again tonight. She closed her eyes in despair as they brimmed with unshed tears.

* * *

The death of her best friend had been extremely traumatic. It had shaken her to the bone and the visions tormented her time after time. Dolefully, she thought that nothing had changed.

Deaths due to plastic had increased over the years. No one cared, and marine life was not a priority to anyone. All that humans cared about was how they could exploit the vast abundance of the deep blue.

Engrossed in my thoughts, I was interrupted by a cacophony of shrill clicks and whistles and splashing of tails in water. A brutal incident of a human-induced massacre in our waters had spread like wildfire and reached us. Anger and fear gripped all the members of the vast ocean community. A broken, battered pod had arrived at the community centre seeking aid.

The pod's elders recounted gruesome stories about the countless deaths and devastation of marine life due to humans and their irresponsible, callous behaviour, one of them being throwing plastic waste. The plastic casually thrown by humans had found its way into their homes and many met with untimely deaths as the plastic resembled easy prey to all those looking for a scrumptious meal.

On this occasion, the killings seemed to be for the sole purpose of enjoyment. The humans had chased the pod in their boats and the pod's chieftain had lost his life while saving members of the pod. He was caught in the propellers of a boat as he pushed a calf out of the way, his body was badly mutilated and blood gushed through the wounds, mixing with the water as it sank into the depths. He died a martyr.

The humans had spared no one in their quest to chase and follow, not even the youngest. The pod was reduced to half its size. The ones that escaped scrambled to save their lives. The massacre had left deep scars, both emotionally and physically.

* * *

It had taken the battered pod months to recover and with heavy hearts, they decided that it was time they start life afresh, so after choosing their new chief, the battered pod took their leave.

After the battered pod had left, days passed, and a deathly silence enveloped our world. It seemed almost eerie, no further loss of life, no traps, no poaching. It was unbelievable! There was barely any plastic or ships in sight.

Rumours had started to do the rounds; the humans had disappeared from the world. Curious to know what had happened, I swam to the surface of the ocean. A waterway that was once bustling with ships and beaches that were once dotted with boisterous crowds littering everywhere, had a deserted look. I was overjoyed. *Could those whispered rumours that I had heard here and there really be true? Had humans seriously disappeared?*

I rushed to tell my pod that the rumours were actually true because of what I had experienced at the surface. Initially, they refused to believe me, so I urged them to come and see for themselves, after a lot of persuasion, they agreed to follow me, but still seemed wary.

On reaching the surface they gaped in astonishment. It was a sight to behold! Everyone was squealing, spy hopping, swimming in circles and cutting through waves. Soon it was time for us to return, and as the sun went down in a blaze of glory, we headed home, excited and exhausted but pensive and reflective of how much humans had changed our world for the worse.

Now that humans hadn't been around for a while, the amount of plastic in our ocean had reduced, nets had disappeared and there were no more oil spills or killings. For the first time, there was hope for a better life and a possibility to reclaim our rightful place in the ecosystem.

* * *

A grand feast was organised to celebrate the disappearance of the human race. Everyone was invited. It was an aquatic truce. As we gloated about our triumph, the abhorrent truth behind human disappearance unveiled itself. We listened with feelings of incredulity and consternation as the same story was repeated again and again by the visitors.

Humans hadn't disappeared. But they had been afflicted by a dreadful disease that they called '*the Coronavirus Pandemic*' and it was taking their lives one by one. All of them had been confined to their homes and it was a must to keep their faces covered at all times.

I couldn't help but picture the masks covering their faces, suffocating them, just as the plastic they had thrown into our world had suffocated and killed Elle, a feeling of elation consumed me. It was *retribution.*

"For the first time in years, we have witnessed true dread on their faces. They seemed to be getting a taste of their own medicine," said one of the guests.

"Karma is getting back at them for the way they have treated all the creatures of the world. Now they too shall live in fear," said another.

"The predators have become the prey," I thought out loud. This was met with applause, hooting and whistling from all sides.

Amongst the applause I heard a reprimanding voice that was loud and clear, "We must be compassionate, look beyond our pain and see the suffering of others. We all know what it is like to have lost a loved one and wouldn't wish it on anyone else." It was Elle's mother.

"If we want to live in harmony, we need to have empathy for others. Sooner or later mankind will understand this and a day will come when peace will prevail. As many humans have already understood and regretted their selfishness, they are now taking the initiative to commit their lives to save the oceans and the creatures of the sea. We must give them a chance." Her voice reverberated in the hearts and minds of many.

It was almost dawn when everyone agreed that humans should be forgiven for all the atrocities that had been committed through the centuries. As the first rays of the sun drove away the shadows of the night, under the water too, light had overcome darkness and a sliver of hope rose in the deep blue.

* * *

On land, a new era had dawned. A young girl rushed to save an entangled turtle from a fisherman's net, resonating coexistence.

3

PERFECT STORM

About a year had passed since the creatures of the sea had made their pact to give humans a chance. The year had passed smoothly and not a single story had been heard of a horrifying human-induced murder of some marine animal.

It was rather unusual. The coronavirus seemed to have dulled its impact and the humans had learned to live with it. A lot more activity was noticed on land as well as in the sea, but it was not business as usual. Only small boats and fishing trawlers had started encroaching the inner borders of the ocean.

The humans had become a little more friendly and compassionate, sometimes even feeding the animals leftover scraps. As the fishermen in their boats moved towards land, they would sometimes toss small fish and shrimp into the water.

There was very little traffic in and out of the sea and it was relatively calm. Some huge ships were going on and about their business but they weren't harming marine animals at all.

The creatures of the sea had begun to think that Elle's mother was right and after suffering through the deadly pandemic the humans had learned how important it was to be kind and considerate of everyone and think of how their habits impacted the environment around them.

* * *

Late that season, we spied a huge fishing trawler moving speedily and stealthily in the sea. It was late evening when it had reached somewhere in the middle of the sea, but by then huge, grey, storm-filled clouds had covered the skies, blotting out the moon and twinkly stars.

Cold, dark waves swirled in, turning the smooth waters choppy. They were accompanied by a raging gale of wind that shrieked in monotonous tones.

Angry waves lashed at the trawler, whipping it from side to side like a child's toy. The deck was sprayed with salty water and men slipped up and down.

Harry, one of the sailors, had braved many storms in his lifetime; but they were nothing compared to what he witnessed on that day.

He sat patiently in his cabin penning his thoughts in a worn-out leather-backed diary as his mates scrambled to save their lives.

He wrote, *"As the universe was once a single point, so is my life in this stormy sea. Never have I craved so much for the land, to step in the rich brown soils of home, to smell the sweet scent of the wildflowers that grow on the hills.*

For on this sea I can feel its fury, all the rage that was bottled within, now pouring out. As if the sea has countless tears ready to pound at the feet of man, to open the eyes of he who has not nurtured as he should have.

It is a tempest that screams under unilluminated and severe clouds.

Yet we sail.

The sea pounds at us with its watery fists, perhaps with the intention of causing enough bruising for all the sailors to remember its anger, enough for us to start a sweet melody of remorse and an oath of better care.

Yet we sail.

As the waves rock the ship almost to tipping point, everything I am, have been, or ever will be, is concentrated into a tiny string of moments - as if it is in this very moment that I am born.

The wind is strong enough to pick up a man and fling him to the briny waves. Every sense is maxed out, every muscle already working beyond normal capacity and still, there is no hope.

But I know the captain and the crew, the storm may take some of us, even break some of us, but those who remain, will endure. For we are the sailors of the sea and storms like these are times when we truly discover what we are made of."

He tucks the diary in his belt and scrambles up to the deck.

* * *

Claire and the other dolphins see an old man holding on to a railing and trying to inch forward. Just then, a wave comes crashing onto him and he loses his balance. He lets go of the railing and falls straight into the icy water, where he bobs up and down for a few seconds, trying in vain to stay afloat, till a mountainous wave swallows him whole.

He does *not* surface again.

The other humans are dripping with water and fear is evident on their faces. They keep trying to radio for help but it is seemingly broken. The men scream and plead for help as they hung onto railings and the mast for dear life.

The dolphins watch on in horror and apathy as another humongous wave hits the trawler. The trawler heaves high and low, rocking dangerously from side to side, and finally snaps like a dry twig on a cold winter morn.

* * *

The men's desperate shrieks are drowned by the creaking sound of the sinking trawler. As it nosedives into the sea, we see the few surviving humans jump into the freezing waters; immediately, the pod and I rush in to save them, dodging through the crashing planks of the broken trawler.

We save as many as we can and swim the survivors to the safety of a nearby island.

4

LEFT FOR MERCY

The sun rose high, casting away the cloak of the night and driving away with it the horrors of the previous night. When the survivors woke, they found themselves on a deserted island with the sea stretching as far as the eye could see, miles away from land.

* * *

Something was tickling me, I regained consciousness slowly and realized what had woken me, and it was the waves that lapped softly at my feet.

Intense heat greeted me and my entire body was buried under the sand. I coughed, spewing some of it from my mouth. Raising my head slightly, I looked around. Some of my companions from the trawler were lying around in the sand. Looking at them brought back nasty memories of the night before, so many men had lost their lives because of the storm.

There was a dull, throbbing ache around my temples and at the back of my head. All I wanted to do was close my eyes and lay in the sand till the sun went down.

I heard someone moaning softly, "Help! Is anyone there?"

Closing my eyes, I rubbed my temples. I hoped someone would help whoever it was.

"Help!"

I pinched the bridge of my nose.

"Please help me!"

I let out a long sigh. The person sounded desperate and no one appeared to be helping him. I guess it would have to be me.

Painstakingly, I got up, dusting sand off me. My legs felt like jelly and the hot, coarse sand under my feet made me feel like I was walking on burning coals.

I stumbled around, searching. Whoever it was seemed to have given up. There were no more pleads for help. I wondered if it would be okay if I lay down again.

"Is anyone awake?"

I heard the voice again. I gritted my teeth and tried to figure out who it was. Squinting in the harsh sunlight, I finally spotted the owner of the voice.

It was Larry, a young man in his early twenties who had just begun working with us. He was half-buried in the sand and there were two large red spots on his face. Upon seeing me, he cried out softly, "Max! Thank God! Please help me!"

He tried to remove his leg from the sand- winced- and then said, "My leg hurts real bad, I think my ankle's twisted."

"Lemme see." I bent down to inspect it. The skin around the ankle was red and swollen. It looked quite bad. I helped him dust sand off his body and get up.

Leaning heavily on my shoulder, he stood up on one leg. He gingerly placed his left foot down, testing the ankle. As soon as he shifted his weight onto the leg, it trembled and gave way. The only thing that saved him from falling was that he was still holding onto me.

"Ahh!" He shrieked in pain and bit his lip, almost instantly, beads of blood formed in the spots where his teeth had broken the skin. I led him to a nearby coconut tree and propped him up against it. I told him to relax while I found a few splinters of driftwood and tied it around his leg like a splint with some strips of cloth.

Then I went around shaking the others awake. We had all been lying at the edge of the water. The briny seawater lapped at the sand, very close to my companions. A little way in was a large grove of tall coconut trees. Around us, the glassy sea stretched on for miles. The island seemed to be fairly large and was thickly forested.

Soon, all of my companions were awake. I glanced towards them, they were still in shock and were trying to process what had transpired. They were just realizing what I had understood upon waking; only eight of us had survived the tempest. The rest of our companions...I *didn't* want to think about that. I murmured a quick prayer, thanking God that I was alive.

Luckily, no one was seriously injured except Larry, who probably had a fracture, but almost everyone had minor cuts and bruises. We were all wondering how we had reached the island, when a pod of dolphins swam extremely close to the isle, jumping high and throwing something towards the island. I could hear it falling at the edge, *thud-thud-thud-splash!* I went nearer and saw that they were tossing us fish!

We then recollected that it was the dolphins that had saved our lives and everyone was filled with immense gratitude. We thanked them and collected the blue-green backed mackerel with silvery-white underbellies.

We decided to build a fire so we could roast the fish and eat them as we were all starving. We found some dry grass, old coconut husk, and as many dry sticks and leaves that could be used as kindling and gathered them up.

We then took two sticks from the same softwood tree we found at the edge of the forest, one bigger and fatter, and the other thinner. Ethan sharpened one end of the thinner stick while Mark made a groove down the middle of the other stick to act as a guideline for it. All of us took turns rubbing the sticks against each other, trying to get some sparks. It took us a good ten-fifteen minutes till we had smoke coming and a small bit of coal. We quickly transferred it to the coconut husk and waited for it to catch flames.

Meanwhile, a few others had set up a small kindling nest. We shifted the burning husk to it, we then put in more sticks and leaves. Very shortly, we had a large fire going.

We roasted the fish and had a filling meal. The coconut trees were a big boon to us. We broke the coconuts off the trees and sipped on the sweet, refreshing water.

II

After devouring the meal consisting of fresh roasted fish provided by the friendly dolphins, the most pressing issue on our minds was to make some sort of shelter before the island was engulfed in darkness.

We came to a consensus that we would make three groups, the first team would be me, Larry, Cassian, and Julian. The second team had Ethan and Mark, while Dave and Keith made up the third team.

We decided to go around the island gathering things that could be of use to us. If any of the groups found a source of fresh water, they would light a bonfire there as a signal to the others. We would then shift base to that area. All three teams would go in different directions.

My teammates and I took the route towards the right while the other two teams took the middle and left. Just as soon as we started walking, Larry stumbled and fell.

He collapsed to the ground, holding his leg and groaning. His face was red, forehead crinkled and eyes tightly shut. He refused to move even a step forward. "I think I'd rather stay behind and tend to the fire," he said. "I can't walk, and we can't risk the fire dying."

"You're right," Cassian agreed.

We hadn't thought of that, and since he made a valid point, we agreed to let him stay behind. We created a stockpile of branches and leaves within hands reach of where he was sitting under a tree, and then left.

We had only begun walking when all of a sudden, Julian ran towards the waterfront pointing towards the wet sand. We followed him and saw some stunning crabs, clambering about in the sand and around rocks, their shells decked out in vivid shades of red, orange and blue that looked like they'd been painted on with an artist's brush. Turtles the size of boulders, whose shells had intense green hues, were basking in the sun.

Cassian did not seem impressed. "You made us run after you all the way for *this*?" he glowered at Julian, shaking his head in disbelief. "We're supposed to either be conserving our energy or finding something *useful*- like *water*. NOT *THIS*!"

I couldn't blame him for being testy, but there was no need to yell at poor Julian, who was now studiously staring at his nails.

* * *

We had been walking north in the direction of some cliffs at a steady pace for quite a while but the sight that loomed before us brought the familiar rhythm of footsteps to a halt.

We had reached the base of a massive cliff. A dramatically high ledge jutted out of the rocky cliff. Upon it was a parade of nests, each one made with proud and loving care. A noisy flock of gulls flew over them with watchful eyes.

We decided to explore the cliffside. From the top, we had a clear view of the entire island. In the middle of the forest was a perfectly round clearing with a huge pond.

On one side we could see some huge shapes etched into the ground. They were like giant prehistoric symbols. There were some geometric figures like triangles and concentric circles while one was a stick figure and others resembled animals with extra heads or legs.

The rocks at the bottom of the other side of the cliff were extremely dangerous and sharp. Each one was carved like an assassin's blade, ready to draw blood at the slightest chance. High foam-laced waves crashed wildly against them, wetting the cliffside with its spray. The sea was roaring and the waves and rocks seemed as though they were at war with one another.

It contrasted starkly with the peaceful beachfront that we had been on just a while ago.

We started making our way back down.

* * *

Cassian pointed towards some smoke coming from between the forested area at the centre of the island.

"One of the other groups must have found the pond," Julian said excitedly. Shooting Cassian a quick look, he hurried forward.

We pushed our way in through some scratchy bushes and stepped into the forest. We walked west, keeping in mind the direction of the smoke. Everywhere we looked, we saw green, green, and more green. I looked at Cassian. "I don't like this forest," he said dejectedly, pushing a branch out of his way.

“I agree,” Julian said. “It feels weird in here.”

No doubt that the forest was an uncomfortable place, but it was fascinating all the same. The thick green of the undergrowth was an absolute contrast to the fragile leaves on trees higher up, the bright feathery shapes of some plants swayed gently and intertwined with the strands of others that hung down. Flamboyant birds with rainbow-coloured wings flew in and out of the trees.

Sloths hung from branches and mocha coloured, furry monkeys with yellow tails and blue faces jeered at us from atop trees, their beady black eyes followed us as we traipsed around. The green that surrounded us was abruptly broken by the interruptions of vivid splashes of flowers and the rush of movement that meant animals instead of leaves.

* * *

Soon we reached the place where the smoke was coming from and were delighted to find the huge pond. Tall bamboo trees lined one end of the clearing. The sun had started on its journey west by the time we arrived. The other group had shown up some time before us.

Upon spotting us, our mates ushered us to the pond and we had a drink of the cold, sweet water. Everyone huddled around and started to make plans to build a shelter.

“This is the perfect place for us. We’ll have plenty of water and these bamboo trees will serve us well if we need to make a shelter.” Mark said.

Cassian remarked, “I think it would be better for us to stay at the beachfront. That way it’ll be easier for us to be spotted by any passing ships.”

A murmur of agreement rose amongst the crowd and soon we had decided to go back to the beach. We notched the trees on our way back so we could find the water whenever we needed it. We cut thick green vines off the trees and carried them with us. It didn't take us too long to reach the beach and Larry waved to us as we walked towards him.

"You guys have been gone a long time. Did you'll find any water?"

"Yeah," I said, tossing him Keith's hip flask. "We got some for you too."

We quickly got to work building hammocks with pieces of wood and leaves. Using the vines as ropes, we hung them from the coconut trees. By the time we finished, darkness had taken over and our only source of light was the fire we had built. So we also decided to take shifts to keep feeding the fire. The first shift was Keith's.

Everything settled, we got into our hammocks and discussed about our day. The group that had taken the middle route had a strange story to tell. They said that they had found a sort of hillock which when they climbed gave them a great vantage point to look at the surroundings. From there they had seen the pond and some massive shapes.

"Are you talking about those prehistoric sorts of symbols that look like weird animals and geometric shapes?" Julian asked. "Cause we saw them too!"

Mark sleepily murmured, "It's rather weird, isn't it? This island has no sign of human life, so how did these symbols appear? And the clearing- how can it be so flawlessly circular? It almost seems like someone carved it to perfection."

His words brought with them a strange feeling of eeriness and we fell into an uneasy sleep.

5

SIGN OF DEATH

It was in the wee hours of the morning when a horrific screech reached my ears. Startled, I tumbled out of my hammock. Everyone had heard the screech and was awake.

* * *

Rubbing my eyes, I looked at the faces of my companions, who were gazing around fearfully. Registering the fact that Keith was nowhere in sight, we began to look for him.

We were scanning the area when I noticed something close to the perimeter of the forested area. Going closer, I saw that it was a hand and instinctively knew that it was Keith's. The hand was sticking out of the ground at an unnaturally odd angle. I stumbled back as a tremor ran through my body and I let out a yell, "AAAAAHHH!!!!!"

"What happened?" Dave came running towards me.

This caught everyone's attention and they hurried towards me.

I pointed towards the hand, trembling. "I think we've found Keith."

"Dig fast! Get him out now! He might be alive." Dave bellowed.

We hastily started to dig around the hand, throwing fistfuls of sand in the air. The more we dug, the more we realized that the effort was in vain. Keith had been completely buried under the sand. After much digging, we finally managed to get his body out.

Shocked gasps were heard from the men and Larry threw up noisily to the side. What we found was utterly terrifying. His face was a ghastly white shade, his eyes wide open and his mouth frozen in mid-scream. His hand had stiffened in such a way that it seemed like he was calling for help.

"Who could have done something like that to Keith?"

"Keith was not a small man and it would not have been easy for anyone to take him down."

"If a scuffle would have taken place someone would have heard Keith, he was loud and brash."

We looked for signs of any tussle or fight, but there was nothing, not even a mark on his body. The incident shook us to the bone.

Larry began to shiver and started rambling, "Let's get off this island! We have to find a way out. There's something sinister going on here. How can Keith die? It's going to kill us too, I can feel it, we are all going to die."

Larry's ramblings were like a premonition and that unsettled everyone.

Cassian stepped forward and took charge, he quietened Larry and convinced him that nothing of the sort was going to happen and all of us would get back safely.

"Let's bury Keith. There's nothing we can do for him." He ordered the men to give Keith a decent burial and signalled me to follow him, away from the crowd.

Once we were out of earshot of the others a visibly troubled and perplexed Cassian said, "Whoever killed Keith, could be a dangerous man, we need to get him before he harms anyone else."

We walked back and helped bury Keith. Everyone sat cross-legged in a circle, looking miserable as Cassian and I explained our plan to them.

"For everyone's safety, let's make two groups and start looking for materials to build a raft so we can get out of here."

Dave sprung up and said, "I saw some bamboos growing near the pond yesterday, we can use them to make a raft." This lifted the men's spirits and everyone got to work.

We scrambled to reach the pond and were glad to find the bamboo trees. We then painstakingly cut them to size with our knives.

* * *

By late afternoon everyone was completely famished, so we piled all the bamboos that we had managed to cut and headed back to the beach. As we reach there, we were greeted with a wonderful sight.

The dolphins had tossed us fish again today. Grateful for their help, we picked them up and quietly had our meal, not a single one of us could get their mind off the morning incident.

* * *

My thoughts kept going back to Keith, alone and lost in contemplation, I dig my toes into the sand and flick wet columns of it into the water wondering what had really happened to Keith.

Could Larry's rambling be true? Keith was by no means a small man, that was for sure, and besides, he was an old hand and a trained navy seal who had not lost his edge, fast, muscular and powerful, he was capable of taking down several men alone, a killer machine.

He was not one to get scared of man or beast, had it been an animal he would have dealt with it alone or at least raised the alarm. Who or what could have possibly done that to him? Were we really in some kind of danger or was this a one-off incident?

"Whatever it is," I thought out loud, as a cold shiver ran down my spine, "Something doesn't feel right- we have to be on our guard."

6

PRIMED FOR CARNAGE

Looking towards the horizon, I saw that the dolphins were assessing our every move. I smiled just the slightest, thinking about how they had been helping us.

Deciding not to ponder further and make the most of what was left of the day, I rushed back, gathered the others, and together we went to get as many bamboos as we could.

The bamboos were carried and piled at the beach, then Ethan casually said, "I had already cut the vines to save us some valuable time, but I forgot to take them along, they're sitting by the pond, let's get them too."

I looked at the sky. The sun had almost set, leaving the sky a shade of deep red.

"Well, hurry then, but take some of the men with you and come back before it's completely dark." I insisted.

"Till then we will break some coconuts off the trees," Dave added.

Ethan took Mark and Julian with him and the three of them rushed off and disappeared amongst the thickness of green. Meanwhile, we created a small stockpile of the bright green coconuts and feasted on their creamy flesh.

* * *

Inside the forest, Ethan, Mark and Julian had lost their way. A sudden gust of wind had blown out their torches. The floor of the forest was lost to darkness.

Somewhere close, they heard a twig snap, and the flight of a startled animal hidden in the bush - caught the attention of the men, they paused, turning to look back at the dark forest, unaware of the birds that gathered above, their wings forming truncated crosses against the leaden sky in which storm clouds gathered, dark and ominous, promising something terrible and fierce.

Mark pointed at the black branches writhing like the arms of a monstrous beast. A cold breeze blew, chilling the men to their bones. They were in a trance like state, affixed to the spot, unable to move even an inch.

The men felt a strange force holding them back it was almost like an impenetrable tangle that was barring them, not allowing them to flee, inhibiting their escape and trapping them within the wilderness colonized by ravenous, bestial nightmare-creatures.

The howls of the creatures only grew louder and louder. They were terribly close.

* * *

Overhead, a curtain of black sprinkled with twinkling stars had been pinned against the sky.

"What's taking them so long?" muttered Cassian agitatedly.

We walked a little way into the forest but no one had it in them to go all the way to the lake at night, especially after what had transpired yesterday. Instead, all of us called their names from the edge of the forest till our throats are hoarse, but we received no response. Fearing the worst, we headed back to the beachfront and huddled together around the fire and tried to fall asleep.

* * *

As soon as the first rays of dawn broke through the clear sky on the edge of the horizon, we were up. With a nice and sturdy bamboo in each one's hand, we set off into the forest to find the men. We headed straight to the pond not knowing what to expect.

The area looked undisturbed and serene, the exact same as we had left it the day before, nothing seemed to have transpired at night. Heaving a sigh of relief, we assumed that the men, not wanting to risk coming back, thought that it would be best to stay put since the sun had gone down and a thick black blanket had enveloped the forest.

"MARK!"

"ETHAN!"

"JULIAN!"

We called out their names and tried to find a trail of footsteps that would give us some clue as to where they had decided to spend the night.

After walking deeper into the thicket for a few meters, a filthy stench filled the air. It felt as though an animal had died and its corpse was rotting somewhere close by. Trying to locate the source of the smell, Dave pushed ahead and then screamed.

He had slipped and fallen into a puddle- A crimson red puddle. We gathered around him and I gagged at the smell, throwing up.

Dave sat in the puddle, frozen with shock; his hands and legs completely covered in blood. He looked down at himself and then at us.

Droplets fall from the trees above us and as I look up to see the source of it. A drop falls down the nape of my neck and slips down my back, then another drop - and then another. I momentarily look at the others before turning my gaze up again and seeing that droplets of blood had covered our heads, necks, and shoulders.

The three men who had gone to get the vines were now hanging upside down from a tree with those very vines, blood trickling down from their severed heads.

Cassian screeches in anger, "I am not going to spare whoever is responsible for this, they are going to pay dearly," My thoughts momentarily flicker back to Keith's ashen face. I shudder inwards but quickly collect my thoughts and compose Cassian.

With great difficulty we manage to climb the tree and cut the vines loose, the bodies come crashing down. *What kind of a creature could have done something like this? What was going on in this forest?* I wondered.

Once we managed to get the bodies down, one look at the badly mutilated corpses, and it was amply clear to every man standing around - there was definitely something inhuman after us. It was targeting us one by one with the intention of not just maiming, but killing.

The instinct to survive in this extreme environment was now more pronounced than ever, we decide to leave our dead mates behind because there was nothing we could do for them; and if we did not want to find ourselves with the same fate, then we had to get out of here - and quick. Heart pounding wildly and adrenaline racing, we grab Dave, the cut vines and sprint back to the beach.

Larry drags himself over and exclaims, "What happened! Where are the others? And what happened to you, Dave?!"

"All of them are dead, and if we want to stay alive, let's get this raft made and get out of here. There's no time to lose!" blurts Dave.

On hearing this Larry pales and collapses to the ground, Dave assures him that he will not let anything happen to him but no one will babysit him and that he will have to collect himself and help with getting the raft built- it was the only way to survive.

All of us work at lightning speed, tying together the sticks of bamboo and joining them. We give it all we have and manage to build a small raft. By the time we are done, it is dusk, and the raft is ready to sail.

We immediately push it into the water, but as luck would have it, we realize the tide would set in only after midnight, and so we wait, praying that we can make it out of this deadly island alive.

Just then Larry spots the dolphins hooting at us. It seemed to him as if they had understood that our lives were at risk and were telling us to get the raft into the water and that they would help us stay adrift.

At this point, we were ready to do anything to get off the island, so even though we thought Larry was becoming delusional and didn't entirely believe him, we went along with it.

We took their '*cue*' as Larry insisted on calling it, and wade in, one step at a time. Breathing deep and gasping, I hobble in further and after a few minutes, my legs feel numb and hard, like they're going to break off my body.

I take a few deep breaths, hoping that it will offer some warmth before I dunk my entire body under. My breath quickens and I slip into the water. I let out a muffled yell underwater. I hear loud splashes and know that the others too, have entered the water. The sudden temperature change feels like an electric shock, but now's no time to make a fuss.

My companions and I tug at the raft leading it deeper into the open, swimming hard, trying to adjust to the temperature of the water and bring some heat back into our bodies.

Once in fairly deep waters, we clamber onto the raft, and using bamboos, try to row. However, neither the wind nor the current is in our favour. It kept trying to push us back to the island, like it wanted us to suffer the same fate as our crewmates.

Tempers soon begin to rise, and Cassian roars at Larry who had curled up into a small, miserable ball. When we had almost given up, a pod of dolphins suddenly appeared and helped us push the raft deeper into the sea, pushing it with their rostras.

Minutes turned to hours as we sailed, we had lost sight of the perilous island about an hour ago. We drifted that way for a long time, cold, wet and hungry, till we came across a ferry.

"Finally!" Dave muttered under his breath.

We started to yell and waved wildly at them in the hopes of being seen. Much to our relief, a crewmember notices the torn shirt that we had been using as a sail and stops the ferry, they throw us some lifebuoys and send a lifeboat to rescue us.

Just as we were about to get onto the boat, a young dolphin of the pod brought us some sea flowers. We were completely taken aback by their sweet gesture and our hearts were filled with emotion.

My eyes brim with tears and Cassian reaches out and strokes the dolphin. Waving goodbye to the dolphins, we get onto the ferry. Larry is promptly given medical attention and we are taken back to the safety of our homes.

7

THE TRAP

Through the following weeks, Dave would come with some men to feed and play with the younglings. After a few days, the young dolphins bonded well and would expectantly wait for the men to come every single day.

On hearing the motorboats they excitedly jumped high up and splashed down into the water to grab their attention.

On one such day, the dolphins decided to show their newfound friends their secret hideout and guided them to a very secluded and almost magical part of the sea where the tepid, glassy emerald waters caressed a rocky backdrop covered with dense foliage, filled with the warble and chirp of birds, untouched and pristine, where the air had the tang of salty freshness that was archetypal of the ocean around that area.

Tucked away at the back of the rocks was a hidden cove that provided the best gateway for small sea creatures and the water was deep enough even for dolphins to catch easy prey and the younglings often visited the cove.

As Dave and his men approach the area in a small boat, they are awestruck with the beauty that surrounds them, they could hear the reverberating cries of the gulls as they circled over them and the dolphins, searching for a morsel and a landing.

Some of the adult dolphins too, would accompany the youngsters to watch over them as they swam alongside the humans.

Sometimes they would decide to give the humans a ride on their backs, diving in and out of the water at a fast pace.

* * *

It wasn't long before the men won our trust and we started sending the youngsters alone. One day, they left as usual, but did not return till late evening. Worried as to what had happened, the pod quickly rushed to their customary meeting spot.

When we reached there, we could not believe our eyes. Only three out of the five young dolphins were to be seen. On seeing us they let out a series of rapid clicks, calling for help.

The pod split up into two groups, one rushed to free the trapped dolphins and the other to look for the missing ones. As we swam closer to the trapped dolphins we realized that freeing them would not be easy, it was a trap laid out by humans which invariably led to the death of the one trapped.

Where were the humans and the other two young dolphins? Had something sinister transpired? Were the humans in trouble too? My mind raced with a million thoughts. The dolphins were placed up against the rocks and trapped by a loose net and were struggling in vain to get out. The only thing that was keeping them alive was that the net was secured high enough for them to be able to rise to the surface for a breath.

They splashed their tails and called out in distress. We tried and tried, did all we could, but nothing seemed to work. At a distance, we spotted a pod of orcas passing by and our commotion had caught their attention, curious to know what was going on, they sent two orcas towards us, one of them was Springer, a female in her early twenties and Spirit, one of her two young calves.

We tried to get Addison, Mabel and Jace out of the trap not knowing the exact intention of the orcas. Two of our pod members braved up to meet them, however, our fears dissolved almost immediately as we realized they had come in peace and only wanted to help.

We explained the situation to them, and shortly, we had the entire pod of the orcas were there to help us. With the extra burst of brute force, our confidence increased. Together we positioned ourselves strategically and started tugging at the net. We tugged and tugged but just could not get the younglings free. After struggling for under an hour, weary and drained as we were about to give up, Cecilia hit upon a plan, the largest of the orcas would splash their tails as hard as they could against the water and try to dislodge the net from the rock where it had been fastened with long nails and the rest of us could try and pull the net at the same time.

We did this until cracks appeared on the rock where the nails had been embedded, however, it would still not give way. We tugged at the net again and again until everyone was bushed and exhausted. We shook our heads in sorrow and we were about to surrender things to fate when Elle's mother swam up to us, she said loud and stern, "You only fail when you stop trying," which gave us a jolt and sprung us back into action.

We all looked at her, she had a glow around her that seemed to emit a positive aura that we all soaked in. With renewed energy and determination, all of us decided to give it another try. Huddling together we decided to pound our tails together to create waves that would beat on the cracks and break them so, together with the orcas, we all pounded our tails furiously against the water at the same time, creating large waves that lashed at the cracks in the rock, after a few tries our efforts finally paid off and the rock was blown to smithereens. The nails too had come off and with much effort and help from the large orcas, we managed to set the younglings free.

In this time of difficulty, we had formed a bond with the orcas that was going to last forever. We thanked them for their help and promised to pay back the favour when the time came; with barks to gobbles, they bid us adieu and went their way. Exhausted beyond measure, we swam back to our homes, praying all the way for the safety of the other two missing dolphins.

8

WHISPER IN THE CHASM

Addison and Mabel's lips quivered uncontrollably, letting out just muted sobs as Jace slumped his shoulders and swam round and round with slow, hesitating movements. All three of them were tongue-tied and could not speak.

Little did they know that every moment of their silence would cost Leo and Cora dearly, we just had to know what happened that morning. After much goading, Addison revealed the ugly truth between sobs.

Dave, one of the wreck survivors had come with his men, and, as was custom the younglings swam to them. None of them suspected that there could be a sinister plan brewing in their minds, so while some of the men swam and played with Addison, Mabel, and Jace; another three took Leo and Cora into the bay behind the rocks. While the dolphins played and frolicked around unknowingly, Dave set out his two extremely well-planned traps.

The men knew too well how to get the unsuspecting young dolphins into the trap. They had practised and rehearsed how and what each one was supposed to do. The group was to be split and the youngest ones would be captured first, in the meanwhile some other men would trap the slightly older ones in a net and then come to get them the next day.

As planned, Addison, Mabel, and Jace were led straight towards the rocks where the men had previously planted the traps such that once inside, they would not be able to get away. The heavy nets fell onto them as soon as they swam close to the rocks. They were confined to a corner and the net cut into their delicate skins.

Thankfully their wounds weren't too deep and they would heal without leaving scars. They were so stunned and taken aback by the deceit that they were unable to move. Grief and fear engulfed them as they realized they had been cheated and trapped by the ones they thought had loved them so dearly, unable to escape the net, they gave into their fate all too soon.

Dave instructed his men to first take Leo and Cora and later Addison, Mabel, and Jace. The mask had fallen, and Dave's true nature came through, hidden behind his innocent face and sweet smile was the heart of a ruthless monster.

After Addison finished narrating the story, they questioned her, again and again, to make sure that she had not made a mistake, but her story did not change. The dolphins could not believe what they just heard.

A sickening feeling of absolute disgust and animosity came over the entire dolphin community. The humans had cheated them once again, even after they had saved their lives, trusted them, and helped them so much they returned to their old ways. Addison, Mabel and Jace had no idea where Dave and his cronies had taken Leo and Cora.

We were deliberating about what we could do, when all of a sudden Frisky the turtle appeared like a shining ray of hope, bouncing in as fast as he could. The information he brought with him was priceless and the chief of the pod rewarded him with some treats.

9

SKY FULL OF STARS

A plan is made- there's no time to lose. Frisky hurriedly rushes towards the shore, pushing with all his might against the strong currents that kept sweeping him deeper into the sea. He kept wishing and praying all the way that Lyra would be waiting to meet him at the shore.

A few seconds here and there could mean the difference between life and death for the captured young dolphins. The plan depended greatly on her being able to find out the location of the youngsters.

When he reached the shore, he breathed a sigh of relief. Lyra was heading a beach cleanup. Strands of her golden hair blew lightly in the wind as she stood giving instructions. She had the same fiery temperament as the day he had first met her- it was the day he had been completely entangled in a ghost net. It had wrapped around his neck so tightly that it dug into his flesh.

Lyra was much younger then. She was on a boat with her father when she spotted Frisky drifting exhaustedly, tugging along with him a huge bundle of netting. Without a moment's hesitation, she dived into the water and swam close to him. He was completely terrified and tried his best to swim away, but she spoke to him in soft, kind tones and calmed him.

She then helped him to swim closer to the boat, where her father pulled them up onto their small boat. Lyra realized that not only had the net cut badly into Frisky's neck but one of his flippers was damaged too; she wasted no time at all and painstakingly cut the net from around his neck making sure not to hurt him any more than he already was.

After managing to free him she even cleaned his wounds and applied an ointment to help the cuts heal faster, but not much could be done to heal the damaged flipper, so her father suggested that they carry him back to the marine centre where he could be given proper medical care and attention till he recovered and was fit to be released.

She wrapped him in a blanket and the father-daughter duo sped back home with little Frisky in tow. The days that followed were probably the most memorable ones for Frisky. Lyra never left his side, she fed him, nursed the wound and spoke to him making him comfortable in the alien environment.

Very soon it seemed as though Frisky had always had been a member of Lyra's family, the weeks passed by quickly and the wounds healed completely, it was time for Frisky to be released. By then Frisky and Lyra had formed an unbreakable bond.

Since Lyra lived close to the beach they met often and he knew she was a friend of the sea and would definitely go all out to save the dolphins. When Lyra saw him, the golden specs in her hazel eyes sparkled brightly.

She quickly came to greet him. Startled by his tense expression, she asked him what was wrong. "Two young dolphins have been captured. There's no time to lose." He wheezed, and then went on to explain the story of how a web of lies and deceit was played out by the men on the wrecked trawler with the sole intention of trapping and capturing young dolphins.

Lyra was moved to tears and could not believe how inhuman that was. She held Frisky's flipper in her hands and promised to do everything she could to find and save the dolphins. Frisky then explained the plan to her.

Convinced that she would not only save the dolphins from the clutches of the monsters but also bring the culprits to justice, he promises to meet Lyra again after five days and swims back to inform the pod.

Lyra sits at the beachfront immersed in thought, pondering, she asks herself again and again; *How will I ever be able to look into Frisky's eyes again if I am unable to find the dolphins?*

The descending sun reminds her of a last, dying ember from the remains of a once roaring fire. The sand glitters as though someone had painstakingly polished each grain. It felt velvety under her feet as she dug her toes into it. The sky meets the sea at the horizon, a thin thread of blush separating the two.

As the sun dips down further, the ghost-white sea reflects the last rays of the setting sun, turning it into melted gold. The last few glimmers of light brighten the sky for a few moments before fading into darkness.

Blackness envelopes the sky but Lyra doesn't mind. She knows a myriad of twinkling stars will come like an army and wrestle the darkness for their place, lighting up the sky like fireworks.

From the corner of her eye, she notices a fast-approaching silhouette. Turning around, she sees a tall, slender girl. Her heart-shaped face is framed by soft brown curls that fall past her shoulders and bounce as she walks, her sharp green eyes are beautifully complemented by her hair.

Following her closely is a wiry boy with sand coloured, curly and dishevelled hair that covers his eyes. Lyra smiles slightly. They were her two best friends, Alessia and Zane. They plonk down in the sand beside her and she tells them the entire story. Big marine enthusiasts themselves, after listening to the story, they jump at the opportunity to save the young dolphins.

They pour over the details Frisky the turtle had given Lyra and finally find something that gives them a clue to start their search. Frisky had described one of the crew members as one with a long scar on his face. That description fit one person they all had seen; they didn't know his name and always referred to him as *Scarface.*

He was a frequent visitor at the local marine rescue centre and aquarium owned by Lyra's father, Jason, and also helped around when he was not out sailing at sea.

Zane was doubtful and questioned, "Why would someone who cares for the welfare of the animals want to harm them?"

But Lyra had a gut feeling, "There's something weird about that guy." She said. So they decided to check him out. They rose at the crack of dawn and as they got dressed, they could see the sky changing colours.

Vivid shades of yellow, pink, orange and red filled the sky. The sun was a glowing medallion in the firmament when they met at their usual spot at the beachfront. They discussed their plan and prayed that everything would go according to it.

The first step was to visit the aquarium where Lyra worked and speak to the employees discreetly to understand if anyone had seen or heard anything about the two young dolphins. Once they could confirm that the captured dolphins were alive and figure out where they were being held, they would then implement their rescue plan.

Step one would not be difficult. Lyra knew that since it was summer, there would be massive crowds pouring in every day. The aquarium was already short-staffed and her father was on the lookout for some extra hands to help around the aquarium, so if her friends would go over and offer to work, he wouldn't think twice before readily agreeing to hire them.

* * *

Everything goes according to plan and Jason does not suspect a thing. Once at work in the aquarium, they immediately put their plan into action.

10

CHILDREN OF STEEL

They keep their eyes and ears open and start asking around for any clues they might get as they work. Days were passing and there was no sign of the dolphins anywhere, at least no one in the aquarium was aware of anything, the three knew they had to act swiftly or else it would be too late and their efforts would be futile.

The man they had recognized as Scarface seemed to have vanished into thin air. Two days had passed, and Lyra and Zane were starting to get restless. They decide to widen their search in hopes of finding other locations where the dolphins could be held captive.

At the end of the third day, Alessia is on the second floor in a room opposite Jason's office, all alone, sorting some boxes, when she sees a man.

He was the kind of man who had been born in a suit. He held himself like a mannequin, stiffer than the collar of his crisp white shirt, even his hair was plastic perfect - hairspray. Alessia turned up her nose in disgust. She couldn't *stand* men who wore hairspray.

He had the mundane white face- close shaved- with the ubiquitous square shoulders and an even squarer chin. As he approached Jason's office, the air became quickly saturated with a distinctive spiciness, a fragrance that had a mysterious, debonair vibe, but what lingered most in the air were notes of vanilla, tonka bean, and rum. This cologne was masculine in an unexpectedly soft way that reminded Alessia of suede. She took a deep whiff of the scent – it was Armani- for sure.

He rapped loudly on the door, his Fendi cufflinks, polished to a shine, glinting like small mirrors. The door swings open and Jason's tousled head peeked out. The man had a baritone voice. He said something in clipped tones which was not quite audible and Jason asked the man to step into his office. The door shut with a barely audible click. It was all very suspicious. They were definitely up to something.

The man seemed all too perfect, and it made Alessia wonder if it was all a facade over something less stable and less honourable. And besides, what could a man like that want from the aquarium? Or was she just overthinking it? Then she remembered that Lyra had told her that the aquarium wasn't doing too well and that they were under debt. Her father had been looking for monetary support, so could it be that this man had come to discuss financial matters with Jason? He did look very Wall Street, after all.

Curious to know more, she pushes the boxes aside and rushes to the door. Unable to hear a word of what they're talking, she peers through the keyhole, pressing her face against the door. The conversation does not seem very amicable and the men are in the middle of a heated argument with the man almost threatening Jason.

Mr. Moneybags is extremely angry and threateningly brings his hand to his side, where Alessia sees the outline of a gun. Her heart skips a beat. Jason's eyes are drawn towards the side of the man and his face turns pale as he acknowledges the man's warning, he abruptly stops speaking and there is complete silence afterwards.

The man gives Jason a cold look and finally breaks the silence, saying something nastily. Jason resentfully grabs a ring of keys from his desk drawer and then gestures towards the door.

Pearly beads of sweat form on Alessia's head and neck; afraid of being found out, she quickly ducks behind a pile of small boxes that were being used to store fish food, and hides herself as best as she can, hoping that the men would not turn her way and notice her lavender sleeve peeking out.

The door creaks open, and the two men start walking towards the far end of the aquarium oblivious to Alessia's presence.

Whew! She wipes her forehead in relief.

They move towards the far end of the floor, it is a dark, dingy dead-end with no lights, a restricted area where no one was allowed and the only place in the entire centre where Jason had not wanted the kids to venture.

Alessia could feel her heart pounding wildly against her ribs and a thousand questions filled her mind, all at the same time. Thinking on her feet, she makes a hasty decision to follow them. Creeping in the dark, careful enough not to make a sound, she shadows their movements.

A beam of light coruscates through the walls, making her feel like she is walking through a kaleidoscope. Jason presses his palm against the dead-end and a small box-like section of the wall shoots out. Jason twists it a total of three times; twice clockwise and once anticlockwise. The whirring noise of gears follows. It becomes louder and louder, filling the corridor and then cuts off abruptly.

The wall turns, only to expose a large opening with stairs leading to something that looks like a basement of sorts, a hidden lair. Alessia stares with wide eyes and a horrified look as she begins to understand that something alarming is going on under the garb of a seemingly well-meaning aquarium.

Keeping a safe distance, she follows them. Expecting to uncover the truth and possibly the captured dolphins, she follows them deeper into the den, but she finds nothing unusual about the room, it's just an ordinary storeroom, with ordinary cabinets and ordinary furniture. She hides behind a large chest of drawers and watches the men.

They stand in front of a tall grandfather clock and fiddle with its case. They are blocking her view, so she leans sideways to try and figure out what they are doing. She manages to get into an uncomfortable position from where she can see them but all the dust on the ground makes her nose itch badly.

Stifling a sneeze, she ends up knocking a vase over. It rocks back and forth dangerously before falling over. Fragments fly outward as it shatters into a million pieces. The sound of the shattering glass echoes in the room and the men snap to attention. They start looking around and walk towards the spot where the vase lay in pieces.

Alessia's mouth goes dry, she was sure that they were going to find her; she could feel her pulse racing in her ears, blocking all other sounds. She scrambles to hide as the men walk nearer. As they are about to find her, a large pelican that had been rescued about a week ago, walks past them, clumsily knocking over things.

The guy in the suit looks at the bird and snickers loudly. He then motions to Jason to carry on with the task at hand. Alessia sighs in relief and slumps her body. *That was a close shave!* The pelican had saved her today. It would definitely get some extra fish when she got out of here.

By the time she calms down and pokes her head out, the men have lifted a small rug off the floor. To Alessia's complete astonishment, the floor underneath the rug starts to slide open and an elevator appears. It's like a scene from a movie! She couldn't understand for the life of her why anyone would need something like that. The tiled floor had actually slid away! The men enter the elevator, the door slides shut with a ding and it begins to descend.

The floor starts to retract back but Alessia jumps onto the top of the elevator, crouching to make herself as small as she can to fit into the gap before the floor retracts completely. As the elevator moves downwards, she slowly begins to hear the desperate wails of some marine animals and she knows she's hit onto something. The lift stops with a clang and the men walk out, still in the dark about Alessia's presence.

From atop the lift, she watches in complete dismay; marine animals were being held in captivity, sea turtles, sea lions and a wide variety of corals, trapped in little holding tanks. She looks around, trying to spot the dolphins but can't see them anywhere. Suddenly, she hears the thrashing of tails in water.

She stops dead in her tracks and promises herself that she will not leave without finding the dolphins despite the imminent danger of being caught that only increased with the passing of each second.

Discarding her fears, she stealthily moves towards the source of the sound. The men stop at a tank, gesturing towards it and Alessia finally spots the dolphins from a distance, they are thrashing about in the holding tank. Angered and relieved at the same time she makes a wise decision and quietly heads back to the lift, climbs to the top, and with the help of the elevator cables and creeps out.

Dusting herself with a sense of pride, she thinks to herself, *what a good thing it was that I continued with my gymnastics classes, all those years of flexibility exercises have finally paid off.*

She doesn't stop even for a minute, as she runs all the way to Lyra's house to tell her friend everything that had taken place and that she was witness to.

11

SCOUNDREL'S TEARS

As Alessia narrates the happening of the day, Lyra is completely taken aback.

"I don't believe it." She says, shaking her head as tears fill her eyes.

"I didn't believe it either at first, but it's true," Alessia replies, showing her the photos she had taken.

Lyra listens to the heart-wrenching state of the marine animals and the clandestine meeting with the mysterious man, sobbing uncontrollably. It was not something she was prepared to hear. Unable to come to terms with her father's deception, she waits for him to return home that night.

When he does not return, she storms into her father's office the next morning to confront him, her eyes flashing with rage as she sees Jason.

The father and daughter have a fiery dispute that is witnessed by the two friends. Jason finally gives up and slumps back into his chair, hands covering his face.

Never in his life had he ever felt such shame and self-loathing. Unable to take any more of the accusations he decides to reveal the truth. With a pained expression on his face, he confesses the truth, "I'm being forced by Dave!" he says.

"I had borrowed some money from him before the pandemic and kept our aquarium as mortgage. Because we've had almost zero business the past year, there was absolutely no way for me to repay the loan." He takes a deep breath and continues, "Then Dave started to threaten me to do his evil bidding and said that he would demolish the aquarium and build a supermarket in its place if I didn't agree."

"You know I'd do anything to set the animals free if it weren't for our livelihood. I love them as much as you do. It pains me to say this, but there's no other way." He admits, looking at Lyra pleadingly.

Lyra is still extremely upset but she and her friends believe Jason. They know they must come up with a plan to get the aquarium back and also set all the other animals along with the young dolphins free.

The children discuss their previously made plan with Jason, but he frowns and shakes his head. He is not convinced that their plan would work against a demon like Dave. They had no idea how wicked and deceitful he was. He was an extremely dangerous man and Jason knew that he could go to any length to ensure that his nefarious plan would not fail.

Moreover, they all risked losing their lives if Dave or any of his men got even a tiny whiff of what they were planning. As the children leave, he shuts the door firmly and then locks it. Leaning against the door, he wonders what kind of a monster he has become.

He was going to make things right. But first, he had to think hard and fast and come up with a full proof plan that would get the captured creatures back to the safety of the sea and also set him free from the clutches of an extremely devious Dave.

Lyra, Alessia and Zane had to completely re-think their plan to release all the sea creatures back into the ocean. They realize that it was going to be an uphill task and without the help of some more adults they would not be able to complete it.

Another day goes by and it's now time to meet Frisky and brief him about the situation. Lyra meets the large green turtle at the beachfront and tells him that the dolphins are safe and alive; she also tells him that they are trying their best to rescue them and assures him that the dolphins will reach the sea. Frisky wishes them luck and promises to get the pod ready for eventualities.

Back at the marine centre and aquarium, Jason is lost in thought and still worried. *Even if we get Dave arrested and blow his cover, how would we be able to get the aquarium back?*

Glen, a volunteer at the aquarium, seeing Jason so distressed, offers to help him in any way he can. He tells Jason not to worry and that he has known for a long time that Dave would come to the centre to blackmail Jason and keep an eye on him.

Jason looks at him in utter disbelief but he is desperate for help. He knows that he can trust the boy and that he would be an asset to them while carrying out their rescue mission, so he tells him the entire story.

Glen then reveals that on his last visit to deliver some supplies to Dave he had overheard him boasting to his cronies about how he had tricked Jason, gotten control of the aquarium, and made Jason do all the dirty work of smuggling sea creatures and his plan to eventually sell them to a buyer in the entertainment industry.

Dave's reputation travelled before him, and everyone knew that it was best to keep out of his business. Glen was not an exception. He too, was petrified of Dave and did not want to be at the receiving end of his wrath and so, had kept his lips sealed.

Sensing a ray of hope, Jason blurted, "Do you know where the aquarium papers are? We need the papers. Once we have them, we'll be out of Dave's clutches."

Much to his surprise and relief, Glen nods and says, "You're in luck. I do know where he keeps them. It's in a huge metal safe and only Dave has the keys, but I know one of his men. I'll try and get them for you."

Jason, filled with gratitude and respect, walks towards Glen and envelops him in a brief but tight hug.

12

MADE OF BROKEN THINGS

Two days later Glen struts into Jason's office. "Got it!" he says cheerfully, waving the papers. He has kept his promise.

With the aquarium papers safely in Jason's hand, the time had come for all the creatures to be released back into the water where they truly belong.

Everyone decides to meet at Zane's house albeit separately, since they suspect that Dave's men have been keeping a watch on Jason and Lyra's house. Lyra and Alessia meet up halfway and walk to Zane's house.

When Glen walks in through the back door, the three kids are huddled together sketching out the plan. Jason comes a little later pretending to pick his daughter from her friend's house, just in case he was being followed by one of Dave's men.

Once in the dining room, they draw the curtains tightly shut and grab a steaming cup of coffee each. They sit around a wooden table and put in the last bits to draw out their strategy and make a list of the equipment that they can use to transport the marine animals.

Each one is entrusted with a task; finally, Jason pulls out a large folded paper from his overcoat pocket- it's a detailed map of the island town. All of them pour over it, tracing the best possible routes from the marine centre to the sea.

They need to be extremely careful and avoid suspicion at all costs; they all agree that taking the back roads through the forest would be most preferable, the one parallel to the freeway, knowing that it would take longer, but that it was the only route that would draw little to no attention from the on looking eyes of curious travellers.

They concur that taking all the animals together would be a risky affair and instead opt to take the dolphins separately. Just in case Dave's men get a whiff of what was afoot, the truck with the other sea creatures would create a diversion and give Jason time to get the dolphins to safety.

During the course of planning out the nitty-gritty details, they realize that they cannot carry out the plan alone and need more hands. Glen gets to work quickly, calling some of his friends and explaining the situation to them, asking them for help and to maintain absolute secrecy. The lives of innocent creatures were at stake! The boys don't need much convincing as they too want the poor trapped creatures to be saved and readily agree to help.

The boys reach Zane's place in a trice. Each and every person in the room goes over the plan, reviewing and reconsidering each step. After discussing at great lengths till late evening, they settle on a single plan of action.

The rescue operation will take place at night, and they plan to get things over quickly. Glen and his band of boys would split into two; one group would collect all the precious corals and hide them at Glen's house so they could later be handed over to the environmental agencies that would transplant them onto reefs and help with reef restoration.

The other group would use the equipment in the aquarium and load the small creatures in their tanks onto a large truck; and then using the back roads to avoid being found out, drive straight to the beach where they could release the animals safely into the water.

The dolphins would be taken separately by the kids and Jason. This was going to be tricky as the dolphins would need to be kept wet and would have to be lifted and transported in slings.

The kids decide that they would keep some buckets of water handy so that the dolphins could be kept covered by wet cloths the entire time and that would prevent their skin from drying out.

To avoid any suspicion, Jason under the guise of a delivery truck driver would get in a large-sized delivery truck through the basement and drive it right into the secret den where the dolphins were held captive.

Lyra starts to roll her eyes upwards, and gives her father a despairing look, there was so much she did not know about her own father. Jason looks away, not wanting to meet his daughters gaze and continues to explain the plan.

Once the dolphins are loaded into the truck, he, along with the children, would drive out of the basement, straight to the creek where the dolphins could be released into the ocean easily. All of them split up and agree to meet at the aquarium making sure none of them is followed or seen.

13

OUTRUN THE FURY

Later that night, the plan is carried out to the tee. The corals are the first to be shifted. They are taken away to the safety of Glen's tiny one-room apartment.

Next, one truck is quickly loaded with all the other animals except the two dolphins and sent off with Glen as per the plan. Glen manages to reach the beach with no mishaps and with the help of his friends starts to set the animals free; at a distance the pod watches eagerly, waiting to welcome their youngsters.

Meanwhile, Jason manages to get the truck in without any suspicion and together with the children, manages to load Leo and Cora, who are already in slings, into the other truck, where they also remember to keep small buckets of water that can be used to keep the dolphins cool.

Jason takes his place behind the wheel and the children sit in with the dolphins.

"All set?" he asks.

Amidst a chorus of *yes,* he murmurs a quick prayer, steps on the accelerator and they speed away into the darkness.

Scarface, Dave's aide, spots the two trucks leave the aquarium grounds in the dead of the night. Knowing Jason's fondness for sea creatures all too well and his reluctance to be part of their notorious business, he suspects something is amiss and informs Dave, "Why would two trucks leave the aquarium when there are no deliveries scheduled? And that too in the dead of the night! Unless Jason has decided to betray us and save the cash dispensers."

"Hah! The little fool won't dare to cross me. I have his neck in my hands. His precious little aquarium papers are in my clutches. But don't let them out of your sight." He says mockingly and the line goes dead.

Taking the keys of the safe out of his well-tailored trouser pocket, Dave flings them over to one of his men and orders him to get the papers. "I'll teach him not to mess with me."

The man hurriedly rushes out, looking like a deer caught in the headlights as Dave holds his hand out for the papers. "They're gone."

"What do you mean, gone?" Dave asked, his eyes flashing angrily.

"What I said: they're gone. I have no idea where they are, or how they disappeared," Jordan said, shrugging.

It was the wrong thing to do. Immediately, Dave's cheeks flushed, and his facial muscles became rigid as he stomped towards him. Grabbing him by the collar, he jerked him close to his face, gritting his teeth as he said, "I had entrusted you with the responsibility of keeping them safe," his voice slowly grew louder, "I told you that they could try and steal them!" Now he was close to screaming, "I TOLD YOU THAT IF YOU LET THEM–" His sentence was cut off by the sound of knocking. Throwing Jordan to the ground, he straightened his suit and began walking towards the door. Directly before he reached it, he spun around and bitingly remarked, "I'll deal with you later."

It was Scarface at the door. He whispered into Dave's ears. Dave's already flushed face turned crimson. Enraged, he walked into his cabin, Scarface follows quietly behind, shutting the door after him with a soft click.

Exactly ten minutes later Dave gets into an SUV and drives out at full speed, his men following suit. They reach the aquarium, only to find that not a single animal had been left behind. "Months of hard work down the drain. That emotional fool." He bangs his fist against the wall. The men freeze with fear, the last time something like this happened, there was one man less in the gang. They quietly waited for orders from the boss.

Dave knew that the only way to save the creatures would be to take the animals to the beach and free them, so, moving swiftly he and his henchmen rush to the beach. On reaching the beach, from a distance, he spots Jason's delivery boy, Glen, with a couple of other boys releasing the last of the Leatherback turtles into the water.

Fuming and muttering expletives he bangs his fist on the dashboard and clenches his jaw; jumping out of the car, he hurtles towards the boys as fast as he can.

On seeing Dave and his men, Glen and the boys make a dash for it, running like the wind, but the boys are no match for the hardened criminals. None of them escape. Quickly rounded up, they huddle together, trembling, their hearts racing and barely letting out a breath, as they stare at Dave and his men with pleading eyes.

Dave is engulfed with fury, eyes blazing and his breathing heavy, as he realizes that Jason had indeed found the courage to go against him and had taken off with the dolphins in the other truck, using Glen as a diversion to buy time. Dave grabs hold of one of the boy's neck and starts to squeeze it hard and the boy faints with fear. Afraid and scared for their lives, the boys spill the beans and tell Dave that Jason and the kids are headed to the creek to free the dolphins. The boys are then mercilessly beaten up and left half-unconscious on the beach.

14

THE CREED OF THE WICKED

Jason and the children manage to navigate through the twisty roads and reach halfway when they spot Dave and his men hot at their heels.

The chase starts to get and Dave's car closes in on Jason, its powerful headlights were burning holes in the back of Jason's truck. Trying his best, he swerves onto a muddy road, a shortcut to the creek. A grave mistake, but the only thing he could think of to get Dave off his back.

A stream of water had made the mud on the road damp and the truck moves at the speed of a snail. The wheels skid on the mud and get stuck, panic grips Jason as he tries to accelerate, but the wheels dig in deeper.

Dave stops when he sees Jason's truck skidding wildly and does not follow him onto the road, fearing, that if he went down the muddy road, his car too, would get stuck in the damp mud. Instead, he decides to move ahead and take the next turn onto the road that leads to the creek and wait for Jason at the fork road.

Jason keeps calm and tries to get the truck out of the rut. He desperately turns the wheels left to right a couple of times to clear out a little space. The kids get out and try to help by shovelling and scooping the mud directly from the ground in front of the tires, lessening the angle of ascent. With one more push- and a little momentum, the truck crawls out.

Meanwhile, Glen manages to run to town, panting and bleeding, as he climbs the stairs to the Sheriff's office. He informs him about the desperate situation that they are in and pleads with the Sheriff to help Jason and the kids.

The Sheriff sees it as an opportunity to indict Dave whom he had his suspicions on for a long time and had been keeping a close eye, but due to lack of evidence, was unable to arrest him. The man had always been careful and discreet about his illegal activities and had never left a loose end or clue to be charged.

The Sheriff, finally knowing that he had plenty of eyewitnesses who would testify against Dave, calls for backup and rushes to the creek. Word spreads like wildfire and soon the townsfolk gather up, vowing to bring Dave and his men to the book, and help the dolphins get back to the ocean.

Slowly manoeuvring the truck, Jason gets it going and the kids heave a sigh of relief, constantly checking for the safety of the dolphins and pouring water over them intermittently. They get off the road and onto the main road thinking that they have succeeded in brushing Dave off the trail and he had decided to give up; but no sooner had they reached the fork road, Jason sees the dreaded black SUV blocking the road ahead with its lights shining upon them.

In a matter of seconds, Jason resolves not to stop. "Kids! buckle up and hold on tight. Things might get nasty."

He was going to drive straight into the SUV if he had to, but was not stopping or cowering down this time. He was not going to lose his daughter's respect. He had promised her that he would save the dolphins and no one was going to change that.

Steeling his resolve, he holds the steering wheel tight, his knuckles white as ash, revves up the car, and races ahead to the creek at full speed, barreling towards the SUV. In a matter of seconds, the truck crashes right into it, sending it hurtling upwards in the air, throwing the sixteen feet of gleaming black metal off the road, into a ditch, leaving Dave flummoxed, standing on the side of the road with a few men buried under the mangled car.

For a moment Dave has a stunned look, as though he had been punched in the face, he's unable to comprehend Jason's move. Standing at the fork road he had imagined Jason go pale in the face with fear upon seeing the black SUV, slow down, stop the truck, beg and plead for mercy and on his command get the dolphins back to the basement, just like he had always done; but instead, Jason had driven right into his SUV, not even bothering to look back.

Jason keeps driving till he reaches the creek and is surprised to find the entire town standing there to greet him, shocked and overcome with emotion he gestures to the children to get the dolphins out of the truck and set them free into the creek.

Glen and his group of boys join in and manage to get the dolphins out and into the water. Once in the water the dolphins freeze, they are unable to move. Lyra and her friends understand the traumatized mental state the baby dolphins are in and get into the water with the dolphins and goad them towards the ocean lovingly, with the crowds cheering them on.

In the distance Cora and Leo hear their pod whistling to them, encouraging them to try and swim back. Finally, after much persuasion, the dolphins start to slowly swim away. They reach the mouth of the marina entrance, but before they can make it into the ocean, two of Dave's ships suddenly appear, sealing off the marina with their nets. The dolphins do not know what to do, afraid and confused, they start swimming in circles.

Lyra and her friends run towards the breakwater, calling for Cora and Leo to follow them, drawing them away from the ships. Lyra goes to the edge and yells with all her might signalling to the dolphins that they would have to jump over the nets, it would be the highest jump they would ever make, but also their only chance at freedom. The dolphins realize that it's their only chance at freedom, they decide to make the do or die choice.

Swishing their tails, they ready themselves to take on the challenge. Lyra and her friends' eyes tear up knowing that this would be the last that they would ever see of them, but are also joyous as they have managed to beat the odds and have kept the promise they had made to Frisky.

Bidding them a tearful goodbye, they pull themselves together and Lyra goes back to the top. She recites a short prayer, before shouting out to the dolphins just one last time. The crowds look on with bated breath as the drama unfolds, each one silently praying for the safety of the dolphins.

The ships try to close in on them and in that instance Cora and Leo take the leap of faith and jump over the nets and land in the ocean on the other side, finally free to return to their family waiting for them.

The crowd roars when they see the dolphins finally free and a thunderous applause greets Lyra and her friends as they go back to where Jason and Glen are waiting, Jason hugs Lyra as they look out towards the sea. The youngsters finally meet their pod and there is a sense of great jubilation in the sea. Cora and Leo call out to Lyra and her friends in the distance, and they say their farewells.

15

SON OF A ROGUE

Knowing that their plans have been foiled, the men lower the speed boats into the water and make a run for it. The sheriff and his men alert the coast guards to capture the fleeing boats.

Jason seeks forgiveness from the law and is pardoned as the Sherriff knows that he did what he did under duress and sets him free with a warning because he had helped set the captured sea creatures free. The Sheriff also promises to help him get his aquarium back legally and then rushes after Dave and his men.

As the men in and around the mangled car see the cops arriving at the scene, they start running towards the forest, hoping to lose them. But the cops know their way around and quickly catch up with the thugs.

An unpleasant scuffle ensues. Dave and the Sherriff circle each other. Dave jeeringly says, “No one can catch Dave!” Grinning menacingly, he throws a punch at the Sherriff. Unprepared, the Sherriff recoils from a punch to his jaw with a wince. In retaliation, he strikes Dave in the shoulder with a hard fist and says, “We’ll see about that.”

The fight is short-lived and in no time at all Dave falls backwards with a loud thud, hitting his head against a sharp rock, he lies motionless on the ground. Blood trickles down the fatal wound and the Sherriff leans down beside him, pulling out his walkie-talkie to radio in the ambulance.

He checks to see if Dave’s pulse is still running; when suddenly his hand shoots out and he grabs the sheriff’s collar, laughing uncontrollably. The Sherriff is appalled at his dauntlessness, grabbing his hand and pushing it away, tells him, “I’ll make sure you never laugh again.” And at that moment, still grinning, Dave succumbs to the injury.

The ambulance arrives and the paramedics officially declare him dead. As they try to move the corpse onto a stretcher, the sheriff notices something abnormal about his jawline. The skin had ripped off, exposing something underneath. He then tugs at the ripped piece, only to realize that it is an extremely well-designed mask.

The deception is apparent, and the Sherriff knows that they have been conned. The man they had chased was not Dave, only one of his cronies with a long scar on his face, the real Dave had somehow managed to escape from his hands once again.

How could I have been so naïve? He thinks to himself. Dave, a master at deception, could disappear into a crowd almost magically and no one would be the wiser. *How could I have slipped up? I should have known better than to expect him to walk into my hands.*

Just as the Sheriff was thinking to himself, he sees a bright red chopper with gleaming silver blades hovering above him in an almost mocking way, in an instant it swoops down as if it's going to crash into him, he runs towards the thicket to take cover, looks up and sees two men dressed in crisp business suits look down from their large clear windows of the chopper, smirking at the scene below them.

The red bird takes flight and is lost among the flashing lights and sirens of ambulances and police cars that fill the air. The Sherriff screws up his eyes and watches helplessly as the gleaming red chopper disappears amongst the clouds and the wrecked car bursts into flames behind him.

He knows instinctively that his fugitives have made a grand exit and he has failed yet again. Dejected, he walks towards the large crowd that has gathered by the creek to watch the happy reunion of the dolphins, his despair is momentarily lost as he too watches the pod of dolphins jump joyously in the ocean.

Somewhere above, enveloped in the thick blanket of fluffy clouds, Cassian turns to Dave and says "In a world where money is easier to obtain by foul means than good, and money is power, criminals will rule the world." Don't worry about this, there are bigger things in store for us." "Your next assignment is waiting for you."

"Yes, Boss," Dave responds with a grin. The men laugh as the chopper disappears into the sunrise.

EPILOGUE

A thunder of applause echoes in my living room. "So you see Val, my friends and I did try, and the carnage stopped for a while. We educated people through our marine centre and through the media. Lots of concerned people around the world joined forces to stop the destruction of marine life," I said in a soft voice.

"Then why don't we have any of the dolphins left, I have never seen an orca or a turtle and all those lovely colourful corals. Where has it all gone?" whined Val.

"Like I said, many like-minded people had understood that if we do not stop polluting the Earth and do not do enough to save marine life, especially the reefs that were being destroyed, everything will be-" I was interrupted by little Val.

"Why was the reef important?" she asked.

"Seventy per cent of the oxygen we breathe would come from the reefs. It was our life source. Coral reefs provided an important ecosystem for life underwater; they teemed with diverse life. Thousands of species lived on a single reef. It provided the perfect balance to promote Biodiversity and it held cures for countless diseases. Unfortunately, now it's all gone."

The fulcrum of our lives has to be finely balanced between need and greed, something that was overlooked then. All our fortunes, plans and strategies dissolved in the blink of an eye, when marine life started to dwindle and pollution spread beyond all thresholds.

Time has humbled us and we have learned our lesson, but it is too late now, what has been done cannot be undone. Now, all we can do is salvage what is left and try to rebuild what is lost.

You, the present generation and future generations to come, must learn from your predecessors and not make the same mistakes that we did. Use your time and resources with care and consideration. Think about how your actions affect the environment around you. Because once these two things - time and resources disappear, they can't be brought back."

"Tick-tock, Tick-tock" Xander mourns as the clock strikes thirteen.

"Tick-tock indeed."